THE
VENGEANCE OF
SAMUEL VAL

ELYSE
HOFFMAN

ISBN 978-1-952742-15-6 (ebook)
ISBN 978-1-952742-25-5 (paperback)
ISBN 978-1-952742-33-0 (hardcover)

Project 613 Publishing
elysehoffman.com

PROJECT613

To my grandfather David,
my grandmother Shirley,
my mother Lydia,
my father Richard,
my sister Liana,
and to God, Who makes all stories.

Fracture

While "*The Vengeance of Samuel Val*" can be enjoyed as a standalone story, it is also a continuation of Elyse Hoffman's previous book, **Fracture.** Characters and plot details from *Fracture* might be referenced in this book.

You might enjoy this story more if you read **Fracture** first.

Thank you, and enjoy!

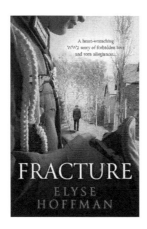

One

S amuel Val's life ended too suddenly one Saturday morning.

The day had been pleasant enough at first: a holy day of rest that he spent with his family in the old Khruvina synagogue. Mama, Papa, and Samuel's three little sisters, all together like always.

The littlest, Dorit, not quite three months old, was swaddled in a pink and white blanket. Samuel's mother Hinda tried in vain to calm the infant as her disgruntled wails cut through the chants of the congregation. Papa prayed louder, blushing so fiercely that his bushy beard couldn't hope to hide his scarlet cheeks. Sam let a small smirk flit across his face. He looked forward to the day when Dorit was old enough to be teased for being the loudest and smelliest baby in the history of the Vals.

Zofia was trying to keep up with their father, sternly muttering the Hebrew prayers with particular reverence. Her voice, once soft and sweet, was becoming harsher as the freshly thirteen-year-old girl was beginning to go through puberty. There was some hope that Dorit would mellow out considerably when she was older: Sam remembered that Zofia had been nearly as fussy when she had been a baby, but now she barely said a word that wasn't a prayer or a curt demand for her older brother to *stop being so childish* whenever he and Cici teased one another. Hinda often said that the future children of Khruvina were fortunate that Zofia was a girl and not a boy. Had it been permissible for her to become a *melamed*, then the icy young lady would have surely morphed into a brutal teacher.

Finally, there was Cecilia, seven years old and brimming with childish energy. She gripped the backside of the pew in front of her and kept trying to lift her whole body into the air like an Olympian, but her skinny little arms were too weak to support even her miniscule weight.

Cici was never the loudest Val, but she was always the most cheerfully mischievous. She had been the most well-behaved Val baby besides Sam himself, and so it was only natural that she had grown into a rambunctious, sassy little girl who could barely get through a half-hour of services without trying to climb onto something or someone, usually her older brother. Once, the Khruvina synagogue had been divided into two sections: men and boys on one side, women and girls on the other. A third section had been added in the middle of the *shul* only a few years ago for families with small children. Samuel suspected that this was partially because if not for Yonatan and Samuel's close presence, Cici would have been an absolute terror. A compromise with tradition had been necessary, and the sexes were permitted to mix in this middle section.

Sam had always told Cici that she was his least favorite sister. He would always regret that he had never once told her she was actually his favorite.

"Hey, sis," Samuel whispered to Cici as she attempted another Olympic feat midway through the Rabbi's reading of the *haftorah*. "C'mon, knock it off, sit down."

Cici let out a little whine and regarded her brother with shimmering blue eyes. "I'm *bored*, Sam," she huffed, plopping down onto the splintery wooden pew and tugging on a loose string in her braided dark brown hair.

"Shhh! Cici, don't say that!" Hinda hissed, her exhausted voice barely audible over Dorit's wails. "This is God's house. Will you tell *Hashem* that you're bored giving Him praise?"

"If He'd gotten bored while making you and given up, you'd have no head, Cici!" joked Sam. "Then again, maybe He *did* get bored and give up since you've got no brain!"

"Both of you, *hush!*" commanded their father, Yonatan Val, pausing his fervent praying and affixing both Cici and Sam with a look that was at once amused and harsh. The two siblings immediately fell silent. Yonatan had always possessed the ability to put people under a spell with only one flash of his striking blue eyes. Sam, who had inherited his father's eyes, hoped that one day he would command the same power when he was the Rabbi of Khruvina. Sam was no less devout than Zofia, and usually he was just as serious except when Cici brought out his impish side. The difference between Sam and Zofia was that when he prayed or read the holy books, it was with a smile and not an expression of pious severity.

But though Sam had cheerfully studied the holy books

until his blue eyes were sore, he was still little more than a congregant trying to keep his boisterous little sister from upsetting *Adonai* with her fidgeting.

"Where's Misha?" Sam asked. His sister's favorite doll, which she had possessed since she was barely able to walk, would usually serve as enough of a distraction to allow her to get through synagogue services without infuriating the good Jews of Khruvina.

"I left her at home," Cici muttered, kicking her legs so fiercely that the couple sitting behind them hissed a complaint in Yonatan's ear.

"Sam, can you run and get it, please?" Hinda begged, her weary eyes flitting from Dorit to Cici and widening with desperation. Samuel huffed because their little home was all the way on the other side of Khruvina, but the Torah commanded he respect and obey his mother, and so he agreed.

"Can I go too?" Cici squeaked, gazing up at her brother with a twinkle in her eyes. Sam would never forgive himself for smirking and shaking his head.

"Nooooo, if I let you leave this *shul*, you'll never come back!" he chuckled, patting her head. "I'll be right back."

Cici stuck her tongue out at him. Zofia sighed in relief. Dorit hiccupped, and then kept right on sobbing. Hinda quietly thanked him. Yonatan smiled and told him to hurry back before Cici drove them all mad.

Sam scurried out of the synagogue too quickly. He would always regret not stopping for a moment and indulging one more time in the crowded splendor of the little building, in the splintery benches, in the frayed Torah scroll laid out on the altar, in the presence of every man, woman, and child of his village.

He bolted out of the synagogue and to his small house, which had been rendered a disaster area thanks to Cici and Hinda's general sloppiness—poor Zofia and Yonatan, the neat freaks of the family, were always driven insane by the piles of stuff that would be strewn across their home.

Sam, who had always found the mess aggravating but not unbearable, would have never thought that his sister's nasty habit of leaving clothes, sheets, toys, and books piled up everywhere would save his life, but it did that Sabbath day. If he had been able to find Misha right away and run back to the synagogue, then he would have already been trapped by the time he heard engines roar and strange voices speaking a language that he knew but had seldom heard spoken: German.

He didn't find Misha, and when the scent of gasoline and the harsh bleat of German commands wafted into the Val home, Samuel abandoned his quest for his sister's doll and peeked out the window.

Sam's heart began to throb painfully against his chest when he saw that demons clothed in black and grey were marching through Khruvina. Some were on horseback, some drove trucks, and the ground troops were swaying to and fro, smoking and laughing like the rowdy lads of Khruvina after drinking themselves stupid for Purim. One word repeated throughout all of the Germans' shouts and slurred conversations: *Juden, Juden, Juden.*

Khruvina was tiny, backwater. There wasn't a radio for miles. Whispers were the main source of worldly information for the people of the village. Whispers and the occasional visit from a Soviet officer who would swing by to make sure that the Jews were obediently providing the State with what little they had, to confirm that their loyalty to

God did not exceed their loyalty to Joseph Stalin. The residents of Khruvina would always be careful during these visits, careful to hide their Torahs and hang up their Soviet flags, careful not to ask too many questions or ask for any information that wasn't offered.

The last time the Soviet inspector had visited, the Bolshevik had offered a crumb of information: he had mentioned something about a pact between Stalin and a madman in Germany. "You'd better hope it holds up," he'd said. "That Hitler fellow, he's a fascist of the worst sort. Medieval attitude towards Jews, too. Worse than medieval, actually."

Khruvina had seen its fair share of medieval horrors over the decades. The Czar's Cossacks had burned half of the village to the ground, and Stalin's disastrous policies had led to a horrid famine that had nearly wiped them all out, but the shtetl had nonetheless weathered every storm. Sometimes, Khruvina's people would feign submission: to the cross, or to the hammer and sickle. For their children, the Jews would pretend to bend the knee, knowing full well that God could see into their hearts and would forgive them for pretending to abandon Him.

The Germans did not call out for the Jews, did not demand that they assemble and kneel and forsake their Torahs and prayers. Instead, the invaders marched right towards the packed synagogue, passing by the Val home and giving Sam an awful bout of nausea. This was different. He could sense in his soul that these shadows given form were not like the Cossacks or the Bolsheviks or any other army that had marched upon Khruvina's soil.

Nobody in Khruvina had a gun—once, there had been

two rifles which had been used for hunting quail, but the Soviet inspector had taken those away several visits ago and declared that if the Jews wanted to hunt, they'd have to use bows and arrows. Sam had no clue where the Khruvina hunters stored their bows and arrows, and so the best weapon he was able to grab as he slipped out of his house was a shovel that had been left stuck in the mud. The teenager moved slowly as he followed the Nazis, nearly gagging from the overwhelming scent of alcohol that filled the air. Soon, however, the odor of gasoline overwhelmed the stench of booze, and Samuel's heartbeat became so quick it was painful.

Samuel ducked behind the kosher butchery and peeked around the corner. A shudder wracked his body when he caught a glimpse at the synagogue. The Germans were circling the old structure like wolves preparing to savage an injured doe, their horses stomping through the mud, the engines of their cars snarling.

The Nazi foot soldiers weren't forcing the Jews to leave their holy house. Rather, they were nailing the doors shut and aiming their rifles at the two windows on each side of the building. The Germans must have struck on the Sabbath purposefully; it would make their job easier, having all of Khruvina's Jews corralled in one spot.

Their job…

Sam heard screaming inside. The din was agonizing, and though the familiar voices of his friends and neighbors melded together into a terrified cacophony, he managed to pluck out the sound of his father and mother begging for mercy, Zofia praying loudly for salvation, Dorit screaming, Cici squealing his name. "Sam! Sam! Big brother!"

The scent of gasoline and alcohol was making Samuel's eyes water. His gaze shifted to a few Germans carrying metal containers filled with amber liquid. They scurried about the synagogue, splashing it with gas, pausing only to pull out their half-empty flasks and take a swig before continuing their work.

"Done, Herr Naden!" one of the Germans said as he and his comrades poured the last drops of gasoline onto the synagogue, leapt away from the old building, and turned to salute their superior officer.

Sam's gaze traveled to the German in charge, the chief demon: a man bedecked in an ever-so-slightly rumpled grey uniform. Dark brown hair, blue eyes colder than the frostiest Belorussian night, and a moon-shaped scar that cut from the bridge of his nose down to his left cheek. In the days to come, Sam would learn the man's full name: SS *Einsatzgruppen* Commander Viktor Naden, known on the Eastern Front as the Beast of Belorussia.

On that fateful Saturday morning, it seemed that Viktor Naden was the only sober Nazi amongst the herd of hooting monsters. He stood rigid, tall, haughty, with his arms crossed behind his back and a grimace pulling at his scarred face. His bright blue eyes disdainfully swept Khruvina, and Sam saw him wrinkle his nose as though the sight of such a drab place offended his cultured German soul.

Naden's eyes flitted to the swaying young Nazi who announced that they were finished dousing the *shul* in gas. The Beast of Belorussia let out a small grunt, as though the Nazi soldier were a student of his whose drunkenness was as offensive as the poverty surrounding him, before he gave a curt nod and stepped forward.

Viktor Naden pulled something small and gold from his pocket. Sam, driven by curiosity, gripped his shovel and crawled a bit closer, trying to see what it was.

A lighter.

"*Cici!*"

Sam acted without thought, without a plan, with only desperation to save his family. He charged from the shadows, brandishing his shovel, hoping to take Viktor Naden's head off his shoulders.

Naden, surprised, dropped the lighter into the mud and drew his gun from its holster. His men took aim, but the Beast of Belorussia fired first. The bullet struck Samuel just above the heart, and the teenager fell to the ground, gasping, clutching the wound.

Sam lay in the mud as pain consumed his every cell. His vision became blurry, but he saw another Nazi hand Naden a different lighter. He saw Naden toss the flame onto the gasoline-coated holy house. He saw the synagogue go up in flames. He saw the Nazis fire upon the few Jews who managed to crawl out the windows, howling in agony as they burned.

And when Samuel's vision dulled and darkness began to overtake him, when ash flew into his face and blinded him, he still smelled and heard. He smelled flesh scald, he heard the Nazis cheer, he heard his family screaming.

He was grateful when he fell into a void and he didn't have to hear any more.

"He's breathing! Five, there's a survivor!"

"Holy shit, that's a miracle...fuck, he's hurt! Here, help him."

Samuel awoke, and the demons were gone. Every building in Khruvina, every house and shop, was burned to cinders. Every tombstone in the graveyard had been knocked down. Every sheep, goat, cow, and chicken had been either stolen or slaughtered. The synagogue was nothing but chunks of burned wood, its old pews reduced to ashes. Twisted, charred bodies were piled by what had once been the blockaded *shul* door.

Samuel sat up and screamed. He tore at his bloody, muddy clothes, ripping the crimson-stained shirt from his body and revealing a wound just above his heart: the bullet had gone right through him, and no one could have blamed the Nazis for seeing the blood-covered teen and assuming he was dead. Somehow, Samuel Val hadn't bled out. A miracle, or perhaps a curse.

The strangers that had found the lone survivor grabbed him, hugged him, offered him comforting words in Yiddish. In the days that followed, Sam would learn that his saviors were members of a resistance group that stretched from France to the Soviet Union. The Black Foxes. When he joined them, he would learn that their sole mission was to save Jews from the Nazi beasts who sought to kill every Jewish man, woman, and child.

The Black Foxes were too late for Khruvina. Too late for the Vals. Too late for Cici.

Samuel broke away from the Black Foxes and got as close to the pile of corpses as he could bear before he dropped to his knees. His friends, his neighbors, his family, all twisted onyx husks melted together into a horrifying mound with screaming heads and grasping hands sticking out here and there. Among them, somewhere, was Cici, rosy cheeks turned obsidian, bright eyes melted.

Samuel grasped at the ground and found something

small and golden. He pulled it from the muck: a golden lighter engraved with initials. *V. Naden.*

Agony became anger, and Samuel Val made his shattered heart repair itself with fire. He would follow the Black Foxes who had found him across Europe in search of the monster who had burned his world.

Two

"Hey…hey! One-Twenty, are you okay?!"

With a grunt, Samuel Val, now known to friend and foe alike only as Black Fox 120, sat up. By habit, he reached for his stolen sidearm and let his striking blue eyes flit about. He didn't have many bullets, but he could probably take out a few Nazis before he had to aim the gun at his own skull.

"W-whoa! It's okay! There aren't any Nazis! I just…you were crying in your sleep."

With a huff, Sam scowled at his traveling companion: a young man, short and small with curly dark hair and great big almost childlike turquoise eyes. Amos Auman was the Jewish man's name, and Sam only knew that because the idiot had cheerfully introduced himself before Black Fox 120 could advise him not to. Names had power. Names were dangerous. There was a reason that the Black Foxes didn't ever tell one another their names, only ever referring to their comrades by their code numbers.

Amos had claimed that revealing his name could do no

harm, for there was nobody he loved that was left for the Nazis to use against him, nobody whom anonymity could protect. Obviously, however, that wasn't true. If it were, Amos wouldn't have even been with Black Fox 120.

Sam wordlessly stood, brushing dirt off of his body and glancing down at the rumpled grey SS uniform he wore, which was splattered with the rust-colored blood of a German officer. The Black Fox had never thought that the sight of Nazi blood would make him queasy, but the last few days had been strange.

It had started when Samuel messed up months ago. He had heard a rumor that Viktor Naden would be in a small German village and had abandoned his post with Black Fox Five. Sam was normally a good soldier, loyal as he was to the Black Foxes and their noble cause, but when it came to Naden, even the slightest rumor of the monster's presence made all thought and reason abandon him. He became like a dog that caught sight of a squirrel. Sam had chased the rumor, hoping it would lead him to the Beast of Belorussia, hoping that he would finally get his revenge.

But Black Fox 120 had been captured before he could even get a chance to get near Naden. His anger had been overwhelming, blinding, and therefore, he'd been sloppy. His sloppiness should have led to his death, but the Nazis that had caught him had taken his cyanide pill before he could bite down and end his own misery.

Samuel hadn't cared that much. He was already a dead man walking, and whether he died quickly of poison or slowly over months of torture, it didn't matter. Nothing the Nazis could do to him could be worse than hearing his sister scream as she was burned to death. The only reason he even bothered to continue breathing was because of his mission, his cause.

So he hadn't broken, hadn't said a word even when the Nazis beat him, starved him, threatened to gouge out his eyes if he didn't talk, if he didn't betray the Black Foxes. Samuel had borne the torture with iciness, refusing to say a word save a few Yiddish curses.

And though a part of him was eager for the Nazis to finally give up and shoot him, eager to join his family and friends from Khruvina in Heaven and leave this horrid plane of existence behind, he had nonetheless found himself praying to God. *Adonai, let me escape this, let me destroy Viktor Naden. That's all I ask.*

Samuel hadn't expected that God would hear his prayers and send an agent. He certainly hadn't expected that agent to come in the form of one of the SS officers that had been torturing him for so long. Private Franz Keidel had been the agent's name—Sam knew that because Amos hadn't gotten the hint about names and had let it slip wistfully from his tongue during an early conversation. At first glance, Keidel had appeared to be the epitome of Nazism: tall, blond, blue-eyed, soulless, the sort of soldier that Viktor Naden would have wanted serving him.

But Franz Keidel had a chink in his Aryan armor, and that chink's name was Amos Auman, his childhood best friend. Franz, unable to harm his Jewish friend, had been hiding Amos on his family farm. However, Keidel's troop had apparently been due for reassignment, and so the imperfect Nazi had been forced to resort to desperate measures in order to save the friend he could no longer look after himself. He had secretly approached Samuel with a plea and a plan: Amos needed to get to safety, and Keidel was willing to free all of the Black Foxes in the small prison if Black Fox 120 would only swear to rescue his friend.

A suspicious offer, but Samuel had little to lose, and Keidel had been willing to lose everything.

Black Fox 120 glanced down at the bloodstains on his SS uniform and grimaced. Their plan had been simple enough: Franz would wait until he was on night duty, kill his fellow guard, and then free Samuel.

However, at risk of Franz himself ending up in an interrogation chamber, it had been necessary to make it seem as though Samuel had overpowered him and broken out of prison without any inside assistance. To that end, it had been necessary to stab Franz and steal his uniform. Sam had endeavored to avoid the Nazi's heart and vitals, but Franz had made it clear that if his life was the price of Amos' safety, he was more than willing to pay that much.

Sam glanced down at the dagger strapped to his side, still covered in a flaking sheen of Franz Keidel's dry blood. Discomfort latched onto his soul as two battling desires fought in his chest. On one hand, Franz Keidel was a Nazi, a murderer, a man who deserved a death far worse than a quick stabbing. On the other hand, Keidel had saved Samuel, his comrades, and Amos Auman. The SS officer had been willing to die for his Jewish friend. By no means could that clean the blood staining his hands or erase his many sins, but *Adonai* commanded Samuel to give even the lowest sinner who showed promise the chance to repent.

Samuel glanced at Amos and felt his pulse quicken. For Amos' sake, he hoped that Franz had survived his wounds. When he had first met Amos, the fugitive had seen the bloodstained uniform on the stranger and asked if Franz was alive. Samuel had said yes, which hadn't been a lie since Franz had been alive since he'd last seen him, and curiously enough Amos, who seemingly never stopped wanting to talk, hadn't asked for further clarification. Perhaps he simply hadn't wanted to know the potentially grisly details. So long as he knew that Franz was alive, he was happy.

If Amos' monologues were anything to go by, he thought the world of Franz Keidel. As annoying as Amos was, Samuel didn't like the idea of breaking his heart. He liked the idea of confessing that *he* had potentially killed Franz Keidel even less.

"Hey, it's all right," Amos said, snapping Sam out of his ruminations. "If you don't want to talk about it, I get it."

Sam rewarded Amos' offer with another grunt. "Let's go," the Black Fox said, and it was simple enough to pack up their little camp. Samuel was used to camping out in the woods, sleeping in the mud amongst the bugs and weeds without a tent to defend him from the rain, and so he felt fortunate that this time around he had a small blanket that Amos had given him. Either way, the forest floor was certainly cozier than the SS prison. He hadn't realized how much he missed sleeping under the stars.

When Sam had staged the prison break, he had taken Franz's car, hoping that if they stuck to the backroads, it would be a short trip to bring Amos to safety. Unfortunately, Franz's long journeys from the Nazi headquarters to his distant farmhouse had taken their toll on the vehicle. The car had died partway through the drive, meaning that they were going to have to complete the rest of their journey on foot, venturing through the woods.

Sam checked his bag, glancing at the few items he had managed to steal from the SS headquarters before he had fled. Some bandages snatched from the medicine cabinet, a pair of handcuffs he had snagged just in case, and a *Tanakh* he had saved from a closet full of stolen Judaic artifacts, no doubt bound for a Nazi pyre just like the people of Khruvina.

Samuel dipped his hand into his pocket, making sure that the personal trinket he had retrieved from the contraband closet was still secure. He felt the wound above his heart, which had seemingly never fully healed, burn as he ran his fingers along the engraved letters of the lighter. Franz Keidel's commanders either hadn't realized that the lighter they'd confiscated from the captured Black Fox belonged to the infamous Beast of Belorussia, or they hadn't thought it important enough to return to the *Einsatzgruppen* Captain. Either way, Samuel had managed to reclaim it.

He wasn't sure if he was happy about that or angered that the little piece of Viktor Naden wouldn't leave him be.

Eager to think of something besides the inferno in his chest, Sam yanked his hand out of his pocket and glanced at his travel companion. Amos had brought along a blanket and a pillow, but otherwise, he didn't have anything but the clothes on his back, including a turquoise scarf that he kept fiddling with, which Sam was worried would get caught on one of the many branches hanging in their path and strangle the poor fellow.

"So, ah," Amos said, shoving their scant bedding into his bag. "Where are we going again?"

"Stop asking questions." Sam's tone was biting and harsh as a winter breeze.

"All right…" Amos said with a wince. "I guess you know what you're doing."

Sam did, to a certain extent. He knelt on the nearest rock and pulled out a tattered map he had stolen during his escape, which he hopcd was still up-to-date. Unfortunately, they were far away from Sam's usual drop-off locations. If he'd had a radio, then Samuel could have tuned in to Black Fox Radio, a station operated by the chief of the Black Foxes, known only as Papa Fox, who delivered secret messages and locations to his agents in between bouts of anti-Nazi speeches meant for the masses. Keidel's office, unfortunately, hadn't had a portable radio that Sam could steal, and therefore he was on his own, with no way to track down Black Fox Five or Black Fox One, who normally shepherded any Jews he rescued to the safety of neutral nations.

However, Sam had not been the only Black Fox that Franz Keidel had saved. A few of his comrades had been in the jail cells of the SS headquarters. They had split up from Sam when Black Fox 120 had gone to retrieve Amos, having their own missions to resume and their own supe-riors to report to. Before they had gone, however, they'd informed him that his best move would be to get to Black Fox 10, the closest high-ranked Black Fox operative, a well-known smuggler of Jews.

Sam had never been in contact with Black Fox 10 before, but they apparently had a good reputation. Paying a visit to Black Fox 10 would likely be the best way to get Amos to safety and to get back into contact with his superiors.

Of course, the fact that he didn't know much about Black Fox 10 meant that he would have to approach with caution. He didn't know who they were or *what* they were. They could be a righteous gentile or a fugitive Jew. If Black

Fox 10 happened to be a gentile, then Franz Keidel's SS uniform would come in handy. If they were a Jew, on the other hand, they could very well greet him with a storm of bullets.

More presently, Samuel would have to make sure that Amos kept his yap shut. That would likely be the most difficult task of all. It seemed that the Jew, who must have been hiding for a very long time with only Franz Keidel for company, was exceptionally eager to engage him in conversation. A little *too* eager. It had been grating on Samuel's nerves the entire time he had known the fugitive, and he was down to his last particles of patience.

"Did you grab anything interesting from the SS closet?" Amos asked as they trudged through thorn bushes and hopped over fallen branches, pressing deeper and deeper into the forest. "What was it you were reading last night?"

"The *Tanakh*," Sam replied curtly, not because he wanted to engage in conversation, but because it would be a sin to obscure the fact that he was studying God's words. There was no shame in reading the Holy Book.

"Oh!" Amos chirped like a child pretending to understand his parents' discussion of property taxes before he conceded his ignorance and sheepishly muttered, "What is that?"

Samuel didn't laugh—he *never* laughed, not since Cici had died, she had always been the one person who could make him laugh—but the clueless fugitive managed to make the ghost of a smirk flit across his face. Not a good smirk, a snide smirk, a disparaging smirk, the sort of smirk that had briefly decorated ever-serious Zofia's face when Cici mispronounced a word during Friday night prayers.

"You're kidding me," the Black Fox said, his tone still steely, not letting a lilt of amusement enter it.

"Ah, well…"

Sam heard Amos' gait slow, and he glanced over his shoulder. The fugitive was fiddling with that turquoise scarf of his, wrapping it around his wrist so tight that Sam was worried he would cut off the blood flow to his hand. Amos' cheeks had turned scarlet, and he looked like he regretted asking the question at all. *Good.*

"I thought you were supposed to be a Jew," Sam said, this time not attempting to mask his disdain. While he was perfectly willing to work with anybody who helped him fight the Nazis, gentile or Jew alike, Sam had very little respect for Jews that had abandoned the tenants of the Torah. A gentile was a gentile; they had no obligation towards Judaic law or the spirit of the Jewish people, and he would never hold them to his own religious standards.

But he remembered how his father would snicker at the arrogance of so-called assimilated Jews. Jews like the young men who would leave their little *shtetls* for Moscow or Kyiv in search of enlightenment. Jews like the fools who joined the communists only to be purged when their usefulness came to an end. Jews like his father's brilliant little brother Avel, who had abandoned Khruvina to become a lackey of Joseph Stalin and the Soviets.

"Those 'secular' Jews, they're worse than any Cossack," Yonatan had said. "Cossacks truly think we're devils, but those traitors are not only selfish, they're stupid as well. They think that leaving us, leaving God, they think that will save them. They betray us because they want so badly to be loved by the gentiles, and then when the gentiles turn on them, they bellyache. 'But I was *different!* I was a good Jew! I wasn't like the rest of them!'"

Amos didn't seem like the sort that would actively betray his people, but he was nonetheless an apostate. The fact that he was even calling himself a Jew was laughable at best and insulting at worst. Being a Jew required work. Being a Jew was a privilege that one had to earn by knowing the Torah and following it.

Sam had a distinct feeling that Amos couldn't have even named twenty of the 613 commandments Jews were obliged to follow. Maybe not even 10.

"I, well…I wasn't really…" Amos mumbled, winding the scarf tighter and tighter, walking slower and slower. "I mean, I *was,* but I *wasn't.* We never did any of the stuff, the ceremonies or anything. Never even went to synagogue. I don't even know if there *was* a synagogue anywhere near my house. My friend who saved you, Franz, he didn't know I was a Jew until he found me hiding in a barn."

"He found you?" Sam grunted. No doubt Franz hadn't merely been perusing the local farms for fresh produce; he'd been searching for hidden Jews, and if Amos hadn't been lucky enough to be discovered by his old childhood friend, he would be ash by now.

"Uh huh!" Amos' eyes glistened in the way they always did whenever the subject of Franz Keidel came up. "I was being hidden by an old gentleman, war friend of my father's, but Franz stumbled across me. He didn't turn me in, of course, and then he ended up visiting me more often and bringing me food and clothes and…"

"You're lucky your friend is a hypocrite," Sam interrupted coldly. He heard a slight *crunch* as Amos stomped on a fallen branch. The fugitive hesitated for a moment before letting out a small, conciliatory grunt.

"I guess…" mumbled Amos. "I don't think he's a hypocrite, though. I think he's just confused."

"*Confused* is one way to put it," huffed Sam. "Confused men ask questions, they don't become murderers."

"Franz *isn't* a murderer!" Amos yelped. "You shouldn't speak of him that way after he saved you and your comrades!"

Sam retorted with utmost iciness. "He didn't rescue me out of the kindness of his heart, nor because he turned a new leaf. He did so to save *you*. His one good Jew. He thought I was *useful*. Otherwise, he would have been content to keep torturing me, and then he would have killed me the same way he and his superiors killed so many. I heard what they did to the other prisoners, Amos Auman. What *he* did."

"He *had* to…"

"No, he didn't!" Sam stopped suddenly, turning and fixing Auman with a scowl that made the fugitive shrink back. "You're not a *complete* idiot. You know that the SS is a voluntary organization. If Keidel didn't want to be there, he could leave whenever he liked. And if he stays after I get you to safety, that proves the sort of man he is."

"And what sort of man is that?" muttered Amos, a slightly angry note entering his voice. Sam shoved his hand into his pocket and ran his thumb along the lighter, biting down on the harsh truth that would have only created discord between him and his charge: *the sort of man who would light a synagogue full of people on fire if Hitler told him to.*

"Here," Sam said instead, and he pulled the frayed

Tanakh out of his bag and tossed it at Amos. The fugitive clumsily caught the Jewish bible.

"The holy books talk a great deal about men like your friend," Sam explained, his voice becoming like that of the Rabbi of Khruvina—firm but comforting. Strict, but inviting. "It is written that the proof of true repentance is to have the opportunity to sin in the manner you did before and refuse to do so."

Amos thumbed through the thick little book, his turquoise eyes glistening with confusion when he glanced at the left page and saw the Hebrew lettering only to brighten with realization when his pupils flitted to the right and he saw the German translation of the ancient text. "So you *do* think he can be redeemed," the fugitive proclaimed hopefully.

"No," Sam said, eliciting a wince from his traveling companion. "There is no redemption for men like your friend, only repentance."

"Isn't that the same thing?" mumbled Amos in a tone that was a morose combination of pleading and argumentative.

"Repentance is a change within the soul," Samuel explained, pressing a hand to his chest and almost feeling the wound above his heart cool as he recited the lessons he had learned in Khruvina's synagogue. Doing so felt good, in a way, like he was spiritually rebuilding a structure that would never physically stand again. "Redemption comes from correcting the sin. Your friend can never correct what he's done, so there is no path to redemption."

"Oh…" Amos' shoulders slumped, his head drooped mournfully, and he began to shut the *Tanakh*.

"Nevertheless, repentance has value in and of itself,

even if the sin cannot be expunged," Samuel declared. "God values repentance greatly, and therefore, if this experience with you leads Keidel to some introspection and he chooses to repent…"

"*Then* you'd forgive him?" Amos' head snapped up with the eagerness of a dog that had been offered a treat. Samuel almost felt bad for being honest when he shook his head.

"No. Absolutely not," the Russian proclaimed firmly before he allowed the uncertainty that had been bubbling in his soul since Franz Keidel had saved him to show as he offered a small conciliatory nod. "That being said…I was reading the Book of Yonah last night…"

"That's the man who got eaten by a whale, right?" Amos interrupted, and Sam huffed.

"Fish. It was a *fish* that ate him. A giant fish," the Russian declared.

"So…" Amos said, and a small smirk was playing on the edge of his lip. "A whale, then?"

"*Whales are not fish.*"

"I think we're getting off-topic," Amos noted with a giggle. Sam bit his tongue and grunted.

"Whale or fish, either way, the reason he was swallowed by the beast was because God commanded him to visit a city of sinners, Nineveh, the capital of the Assyrian Empire. *Hashem* wanted the Prophet Yonah to urge the people of Nineveh to repent lest they be destroyed," the Russian explained. "But Yonah, an Israelite whose people had been oppressed by the Assyrians for the longest time, thought that the people of Nineveh *deserved* to be destroyed. He didn't want them to repent and be given mercy from the Most Merciful, and so he fled."

"There's no running from God," Amos noted.

Sam nodded in agreement and continued: "Thus, he was thrown from the ship of his boat and swallowed…"

"By a whale."

"*Fish*," Sam emphasized, and he could feel his cheeks turn scarlet when the stupid little apostate dared to chuckle at him. Fantastic, now Amos would be teasing him with his biblical illiteracy for the rest of the journey.

"At any rate," Sam said, almost smirking when the turquoise-eyed fugitive opened the *Tanakh* wide and buried his nose in the Book of Yonah. "The point is that Yonah was punished not merely for *refusing* to do as God commanded, but for *interfering* with the repentance of the wicked. *Adonai*, the Lord, He commands us to hate the wicked, but we are not permitted to place a stumbling block on the path to repentance. It is not for me to decide whether or not a man is worthy of experiencing repentance, just as it was not Yonah's place to say that the people of Nineveh did not deserve to repent."

"You know all of this stuff like the back of your hand, hm?" mumbled Amos, lifting his gaze from the *Tanakh*. He sounded both wary and impressed, as though Samuel was a hangman that had just told him the finer details of tying a noose. Sam shoved his hand into his pocket again, tracing the German lettering engraved on Naden's golden lighter.

"I was going to be a Rabbi…" the Russian confessed, and he tightened his jaw. He had never spoken about his old lost life. It would do him no good to mourn what could have been, what he'd wanted. That would only get in the way of his mission. He hated Amos for wringing even that little rumination out of him.

"I'm sure you'll be a great Rabbi when this is all over!"

Amos made it worse when he gave a hopeful proclamation punctuated by a bright smile that was far, far too much like the one Cici would give Samuel when she offered a bitingly fond insult. *You're gonna be the worst Rabbi in Khruvina's history, big brother!*

Cici's scream echoed in his ears. The smell of her flesh burning invaded his nostrils and made nausea and fire erupt in his chest. The wound above his heart prickled, and he tightened his grip on the lighter in his pocket. "Let's keep moving."

Amos had been quiet for the past day. For a little while, this was a source of great relief for Samuel, who was finally able to focus on the path, the map, the mission, and the fire in his soul instead of dealing with Amos' dumb little questions and anecdotes.

But night had fallen, and instead of either trying to pry something resembling a conversation out of Black Fox 120 or simply going to sleep, Amos had plopped down on the cold ground with the frayed *Tanakh* resting in his lap. He wore an expression of severity that did not suit his typically optimistic features. Almost a queasy expression, like he had eaten an apple and wasn't entirely sure whether or not it had been rotten. It was an expression that certainly didn't befit a Jew gazing down at the word of God.

"Learn anything?" Sam asked as he made a small nest of blankets, regarding Amos with a small nod, a note of his regard. Even if it seemed that the section of the *Tanakh* which Amos was reading bothered him greatly, the fact that he was still studying it and hadn't simply tossed the book aside and dismissed it out of hand was, in Samuel's eyes, a great merit.

"I like the Book of Yonah," Amos said, chewing on his lip, winding his scarf around his wrist again. "Not sure about some of the Torah, though…"

"Which part is bothering you?" Samuel softened his voice considerably, like he was talking to a toddler who was understandably bothered by reading about the Tenth Plague. His father and the Rabbi had taught him not to lash out at souls who were bothered by the bloodier parts of the holy books. *A true Jew doesn't just accept all that's written,* Yonatan had said. *Do you know what 'Israel' means, son? He who wrestles with God. That's what it means to be a Child of Israel. A Jew isn't a Jew if he doesn't struggle with the divine. A God who can't deal with questions is no God at all.*

"I wanted to read a little on David and Goliath, and I got to this…"

Amos handed Samuel the *Tanakh* and pointed to the offending section from the Book of Samuel. The chapter where God decided that the wicked nation of Amalek was no longer worthy of life. The chapter where He commanded King Saul to kill every Amalekite. The part where Saul lost his throne for showing the Amalekite king and his livestock mercy.

"*This is what Hashem says: 'I will punish the Amalekites for what they did to Israel when they attacked them as they came up from Egypt,*'" Samuel read aloud. "*Now go, attack the Amalekites and totally destroy everything that belongs to them. Do not spare them; put to death men and women, children and infants, cattle and sheep, camels and donkeys.'*"

"It sort of contradicts the Book of Yonah, doesn't it?"

Amos said. "God's supposed to be merciful, but He orders Saul to kill women and children and goats. And then Saul gets punished for sparing the goats!"

"That's *different*," Samuel declared, shutting the *Tanakh* and bringing it close to his chest, as though to protect it from the apostate shivering before him. Amos' eyes flared with a strange mixture of exasperation and sorrow.

"Different how?" Amos prodded. "God could forgive Nineveh, but not Amalek?"

"Amalek is *different*," Sam spat, suddenly feeling the wound above his heart scald almost as bad as it did whenever he imagined Naden's scarred face. "It's the manifestation of wickedness."

Before the Nazis had ever stepped a toe on Khruvina's soil, the name of *Amalek* had been on the tongue of every resident whenever whispers of another foe approaching had swept through the *shtetl*. In the Torah, Amalek was a physical foe, a tribe which had attacked the weary recently liberated Jewish slaves during their long march from the edge of the Red Sea to the Promised Land.

Amalek was different, however, in that it hadn't attacked the men, the soldiers, the strong, but had aimed for the elderly, the children, the Hebrews' heart. This wickedness had pointed to their true nature, a nature that had mandated their slaughter and made it so that one of the six-hundred-and-thirteen commandments obligated the Jews to always remember Amalek and fight against him. The nation of Amalek was dead, but Amalek lived on in every Cossack, Soviet, and SS man that mirrored its ancient actions. King Saul, by showing even one Amalekite mercy, had guaranteed that the Amalekite curse that was anti-Semitism continued on and festered for generations.

"So…the Amalekites, they're a race of soulless creatures that all needed to be exterminated," mumbled Amos, brow furrowing, tone becoming sour. "Gosh, *that* sounds familiar. Sounds like what the Nazis say about *us*."

"The Nazis are *wrong* about us." Samuel buried his dirty, too-long nails into the paperback, pressing it hard against his heart as though his wound was still bleeding and the *Tanakh* was the only thing that could stop the flow. Yonatan would have disapproved of Samuel's behavior right then: he should have been a gentle shepherd, a wise teacher, explained the nuances of the situation with Amalek in a soft tone. But by castigating God's dictate to battle Amalek, Amos was also castigating Samuel himself, who battled Amalek every day, every moment, whose only reason for breathing was hunting down the Amalekite named Viktor Naden.

"But they *think* they're right," Amos countered, his tone becoming Rabbi-like: soft but firm, a teacher grabbing a wayward student and trying to yank him onto the right path. "By your logic, the Nazis could say they're justified because they think Hitler's some divine messiah and God is with them. This doesn't match what you said about repentance and second chances…"

Sam snarled, shoving his hand into his pocket and grasping at Naden's lighter. "We are commanded to give those who might have a chance at repenting an opportunity to do so, but that *doesn't* mean giving carte blanche to the wicked."

"It isn't about giving them carte blanche," Amos argued. "If Amalek is effectively an ancient version of the Nazis, then fine, burn them, but not their children or their livestock."

"Misplaced mercy is cruelty in disguise," Samuel retorted. "Saul offered mercy to the Amalekite king, and as a result, we have to worry about Amalek's descendants hundreds of years later. Hitler, Himmler, all of the Nazis, they're all cut from the Amalekite cloth. Even if they're not literal descendants, they're *spiritual* descendants."

"This still sounds like Nazi logic. Kill the children so that their descendants don't come after us."

"Don't compare us to them," Samuel hissed, tightening his grip on the lighter so fiercely that he could feel the engraving of Naden's name press into his palm. "The Amalekites attacked the old and young Israelites who had just escaped slavery…"

"So that justifies killing *their* elderly, *their* children?"

"*Ain takhat ain.* An eye for an eye," Sam declared coldly, tapping the cover of the *Tanakh* with his index finger as he quoted the holy book.

"An eye for an eye, sure," Amos conceded. "But that just means hurting the guilty the way they hurt others, not hurting innocent people."

"And if the guilty hurt *our* families? If the Amalekites torture and butcher the innocent people we love?" Sam countered, his anger spiking as his wound burned and reminded him of the last Shabbat in Khruvina. "The *Tanakh* says that when the father sins, his children's teeth are blunted. The Egyptians killed Jewish children, and eventually their own children perished. You might find that *uncomfortable*, but it is *reality*. Do you think that when the Allies hit Germany with bombs, no German children will die? They will, and perhaps they won't deserve it, but their wicked parents do."

"By that logic, then…it would have been good if I died so that Franz would learn a lesson," Amos muttered.

"Yes," Samuel confirmed, running his thumb along the bloodstains decorating his stolen uniform. "And if Franz doesn't repent, then he'd deserve the pain of losing his friend."

"You think I deserve to die, then?" Amos' query was strangely casual, as though he was merely asking how Black Fox 120 took his coffee. Sam shook his head.

"You're still thinking like a child. It isn't a matter of what *you* deserve, it's a question of what *Franz* deserves. If I thought it would be good for you to die, I wouldn't be trying to get you to safety."

"Fair enough," sighed Amos, leaning back against a mossy tree and finally unwinding the scarf from his wrist. "I don't agree: I think that sometimes innocent people do get hurt when fighting evil, like you said about the German civilians, but that doesn't mean you *intentionally* target them just to get even. It's completely evil to harm a child for *any* reason, no matter *who* their family is. Whatever the *Tanakh* says, that's *wrong.*"

"The *Tanakh* has many interpretations," Sam muttered, loosening his grip on the holy book and letting his anger ebb into nothingness. *A Jew isn't a Jew if he doesn't struggle with the divine.* Perhaps Amos was a real Jew after all. "Maybe you'd prefer the Talmud. That's all about interpretation. Interpretation and argument."

"Argument is allowed?" Amos' brow lifted, and he sounded surprised. When Samuel nodded, the fugitive gave a small smile.

"Argument is encouraged for Jews," Sam said. "Get two

Rabbis in a room and there will be a bloodbath. I remember…"

Samuel almost, *almost* let a story tumble off his tongue about the time a Rabbi had visited from out of town. The visitor and Khruvina's Rabbi had spent two hours screaming at each other about the particulars of whether or not God hardening Pharaoh's heart in the Book of Exodus meant that free will was nonexistent. Cici and Sam had listened, Sam with morbid fascination and Cici with ignorant delight. She had giggled as the Rabbis exchanged increasingly creative curses with one another. Then Papa had pulled them away and whispered, "That'll be you someday, Sam…"

The lighter burned in his palm, the scent of smoldering bodies seized his sinuses, and the memory of Cici's laugh turned into a scream.

He gave the *Tanakh* back to Amos with a huff and a scowl. "We're allowed to debate things."

"Ah, well, that's good," Amos sighed, wrapping his arms around the holy book. "If I'm going to be lumped in with all of you, I'd rather be roped into a religion that isn't as dogmatic as the rest. You're not gonna stone me to death just for disagreeing with something in the *Tanakh*, right?"

A part of Sam was tempted to jest that he would stone Amos to death if he kept blabbering constantly, but he suppressed the urge to be snarky. "No, I won't."

"Good, because this book," Amos held up the *Tanakh*, waving it about, his turquoise eyes twinkling impishly. "It definitely gets a lot wrong. For example, while I was reading the Book of Yonah, it kept saying that he was swallowed by a fish, but it was *definitely* talking about a whale."

Sam gave in. "Call it a whale one more time and I *will* stone you to death."

"Soooo…question."

It seemed that their nightly conversations about the *Tanakh* had made Amos bolder. Sam's resistance had fractured, his father's counsel and his inner Rabbi unwilling to leave questions about Judaism unanswered.

"What question?" Sam said, slowing down a bit to allow Amos to walk at his side rather than behind him.

"You're Russian, right?" Amos inquired, fiddling with the end of his scarf. "The accent, I mean, I'm bad at recognizing accents. One time in the Ghetto I called a Belgian woman French and *that* was a shitshow…"

"Yes, I'm Russian," Samuel interrupted with not a small amount of pride. His loyalty had, for most of his life, been with Khruvina and not the ethnicity he'd been born into, but the Russians had been fighting bravely against the Nazi onslaught. Samuel was no Soviet, certainly no communist, but he was proud to be a part of such a stubbornly resilient people.

"But your German is very good!" Amos declared. "I was just wondering why you learned German, how you speak it so well. I took English in school. I could *maybe* get by if we bumped into a Brit or an American, but you're practically fluent. Do they teach German in the Soviet Union?"

Sam's heart palpitated. Whether or not the Soviet schools taught German was immaterial; Khruvina had been a village of Russian, Hebrew, and Yiddish. Samuel knew German because his father had known German, and Yonatan had known German because when German soldiers had marched into Khruvina during the Great War, they weren't monsters.

Those German soldiers were kind, civil. They sat politely in the synagogue during services. They gave chocolate to the children. There were Jews amongst them who spoke highly of their cultured nation and brought books from the great Jewish thinkers of Kaiser's Reich.

Yonatan had picked up the language of the German guests within days. He had taught his son German so that he could read the books that those soldiers had left behind. "Maybe someday you'll go to Germany and bump into some of those men," Yonatan had chuckled. "They said it was nice there."

Those good German soldiers from the Great War had damned Khruvina. Their civility put the *shtetl* at ease. When their countrymen became corrupted, when word had spread of a madman driving Germany into darkness, the men and women of Khruvina, who remembered chocolates and songs and shared synagogue services, had shaken their heads and refused to panic and prepare for the worst. *It can't be that bad. They were civilized. They were good.*

Sam was struck by the urge to burn down the woods about him, to decimate every inch of German soil.

But he glanced at the curious German following him and huffed. "Yes," he answered, and they continued marching through the German forest.

"A QUESTION."

Here we go again. Better to get it over with. Arguing wouldn't help.

"Ask," Sam said, glancing over his shoulder at the fugitive. Amos started winding that damned scarf around his wrist.

"Well," the fugitive said. "I know you can't tell me much, but what's it like being in the Black Foxes?"

Amos spoke with the excitement of a little boy begging to hear an exciting war story. Sam felt his blood bubble. That was a question he had been asked many a time by young rescuees who thought that they had nothing to lose, who dreamed of gloriously slaying the monsters in the SS, who didn't *really* know what it meant to be a Black Fox.

Always, Sam answered that question with earnest harshness. He was willing to accept whatever help was offered, and he would always be grateful to Black Fox Five for saving his life and giving him purpose, but he refused to be the one to bring any soul into the Black Foxes. He wouldn't have some poor, stupid hero's death on his over-burdened conscience.

"Dangerous," Sam answered. "I know what Papa Fox says on the radio, but he romanticizes things. Fighting Nazis isn't glamourous. You wouldn't last five minutes."

"Oh, I'm sure I wouldn't," chuckled Amos, waving one hand towards his feet, gesturing to his own frail form. "Still, does it feel...good, a little? To save people?"

There was an anxiousness to Amos' tone that didn't befit the innocuousness of the question.

"It does," Sam confirmed. "But it would feel better if we didn't need to save them anymore."

"Ah. Hm."

Samuel heard his charge's footsteps become slow and heavy. Sighing, the Russian held up a hand, stopping their march. He turned to face Amos. The fugitive was strangling his wrist with his turquoise scarf.

"You want to ask something else," Sam observed, and Amos bit his lip and nodded, tightening the scarf even more harshly despite the fact that his fingers must have gone numb by now.

"How does it feel to kill people?" the fugitive asked so quietly that Black Fox 120 barely heard him. An expected question, but nonetheless, it made Sam feel a slight pang. He brushed his thumb against the gun strapped to his side and glanced down at Franz's uniform.

"Why are you asking *me* this?" the Russian asked, nudging his chin downwards to indicate the stolen SS outfit. Amos' eyes flitted to the bloodstains on the grey uniform's breast and flashed with sorrow.

"As opposed to Franz, you mean," Amos muttered. The tips of his fingers were purple, and for a moment he gnawed on his bottom lip before he let out a sigh of defeat. "I guess I didn't want to know his answer, and I knew he wouldn't answer honestly."

"And you think *I* will?" Sam scoffed, and Amos offered the Black Fox a smirk.

"I think you don't really give a shit what I think, so yes," the fugitive declared.

Amos' earnest explanation might have fetched a chuckle from Samuel if his question weren't making the Russian's mind buzz with memories. The skin on his hands prickled as he recalled the battalion's worth of beasts he had felled. Most Black Foxes were not fighters, but Samuel Val was one of the rare exceptions.

By no means was Samuel the greatest soldier in the history of European warfare, but Black Fox Five had taught him how to shoot and brawl, and while he still wasn't nearly as trained as the Nazis he fought, the memory of Khruvina's last Sabbath drove him to fight hard, to be ruthless, to make them pay at any cost. His suicidal eagerness to kill Nazis often overwhelmed his more well-trained, coolheaded enemy, and so the young Russian had managed to kill many SS men. Amalekites of every sort, from the middle-aged officer whose sneer became a pathetic plea for mercy once he was on his knees, to the zealous teen who died with a "Heil Hitler!"

The fire in Samuel's soul had not permitted him a moment of hesitation or introspection when he had killed those Nazis in the past. At best, they were obstacles in his path towards Viktor Naden. At worst, they were Naden's agents, his shadows. Their faces blurred together into a mass of darkness, every one morphing into the monsters that had sealed the doors of Khruvina's synagogue shut and laughed while Cici burned.

Samuel didn't doubt that he had probably killed quite a few men who were just like Franz Keidel. He also didn't care. An Amalekite was an Amalekite, a Nazi was a Nazi. All of them, including Franz Keidel, deserved far worse than what he had given the monsters he had killed in the past.

"I don't kill *people*."

Samuel's declaration, delivered with an iciness that could have made a Siberian shiver, caused Amos to let out a small squeak of fright like a mouse that had just realized it was in the company of a cat.

Black Fox 120 didn't give his charge an opportunity to

object to his dehumanization of Franz Keidel. He turned his back on the fugitive and stomped into the thicket, threatening to abandon Amos if he didn't drop the subject and follow in silence.

Amos followed orders.

"A QUESTION."

Amos' eyes glistened. "*You* have a question?! Wow, the world's turning upside down!"

Samuel heaved an exasperated sigh and almost dropped the matter right then, but curiosity and an urge to prove his own assumptions correct made him speak anyway.

"You seem like an optimist," the Russian said, and Amos' smile stretched wider as he clutched at his turquoise scarf.

"Haha! Franz used to say the same thing," the fugitive declared, tossing a blanket onto the grassy ground and sitting across from the Russian, who had already set up his little nest next to a dead tree.

"That's the thing," Samuel said, leaning against the tree and gesturing to Franz's uniform. "You said Keidel *found you* in a barn. Were you hiding there the whole time? Since things got really bad in Germany?"

Amos' bright smile twitched and turned sour. "Oh...I get it," the fugitive muttered, his tone almost admonishing, like he was speaking to a child that had just said a naughty word. "You think I wasn't at a camp or ghetto. I didn't see any real shit, so I'm naive and don't know what's *really* happening. How bad everything *really* is."

"That's not *exactly* what I'm saying," Sam demurred, shoving his hand into his pocket and tracing the Germanic engraving on Naden's lighter with his fingernails. "But it *does* seem like you're a bit too willing to give the Germans a chance."

"Hey, friend: *I'm* German." Amos' chastising tone gave way to false umbrage. Samuel scoffed and grasped the lighter.

"Not anymore," Black Fox 120 pointed out, and Amos' smile vanished.

"No...I guess not," the fugitive conceded, winding his scarf about his wrist tightly and shaking his head. "Listen, though: just because I don't think the whole country should burn along with everyone in it doesn't mean that I think Hitler just needs a hug. Franz, he's the exception, not the rule. I was in a ghetto before I escaped and made it to the barn where he found me. Believe me, I know how low the SS is."

A shadow passed over Amos' face, a familiar darkness that made Samuel regard his charge with a fraternal nod.

"I don't even fully disagree with you," Amos continued, letting his wrist escape from its scarf noose and gesturing vaguely in the direction they came from, the direction of Nazi civilization. "The SS officers *deserve* to lose their wives and children; they *deserve* to feel the same pain we've gone through. Whatever they get at trial when this is all over is too good for them. Whatever they get in *Hell* is too good for most of them. But I don't think you're right about the Amalek thing, the grapes-blunting thing. Hurting normal Germans would make us just as bad as them."

"*That* talk, *that* is what makes me think you don't know what's going on," Sam spat, wrapping his hand around the lighter and gripping it tight, fueling the fire in his heart as his wound burned like lava. "There's no *possible* way for us to sink as low as them."

Amos didn't offer a retort. He merely gave Samuel a harrowing look of disappointment, an expression that mirrored the look his mother had given him when he teased Cici, and she didn't understand that insults were simply how the siblings said *I love you.*

"Never mind!" Samuel snapped, the memory of his mother's face making him nauseous: he hated how Viktor Naden had not only stolen his mother, but his ability to think of her without feeling sick. "I shouldn't have asked. Get some sleep. We'll be at Black Fox Ten's place tomorrow."

"All right," Amos muttered. "Are you going to leave as soon as you drop me off?"

"No," Sam answered, his furious tone melting into resignation. He suddenly became acutely aware of how dirty he was and squirmed: he could feel months' worth of dried sweat clinging to every inch of his body. "I was in that damn cell too long. I want to clean up a bit. Get changed, at least."

"I hope Black Fox Ten has a razor!" Amos chuckled, running his hand along his unshaven chin and wincing at the little bit of stubble that marred his boyish face. Sam nodded in agreement and did the same, brushing his fingers over the scratchy beard that he had grown during his internment.

When Sam had been little, he had dreamed of growing out a big beard like that of his father or Khruvina's Rabbi, but when puberty had hit, he'd found facial hair discomforting. Itchy. Besides, Cici had laughed at him the first time he'd tried to grow out his beard. *You look weird, big brother! Like the Soviet inspector!*

Sam was glad when Amos, whose gaze had traveled to Franz's bloodstained SS uniform, spoke before the memory of Cici's teasing voice could morph into a scream. "Hm... you mind if I keep the uniform?"

Samuel lifted an eyebrow, his gaze flitting from the Nazi's grey coat to the bright-eyed fugitive. "It won't fit you," he said, pinching a small piece of the uniform between two fingers. "Besides, I'd think *this* is the part of your friend you wouldn't want to remember."

"True, but he *did* use it well sometimes," Amos muttered softly, rubbing the end of his scarf between his fingers. "He used it to get me to safety, to protect me. Even something as bad as an SS uniform can be good in the right hands. Hey, *you're* using it."

The feeling of being covered in muck intensified, and a wave of nausea so intense that it made Samuel want to vomit struck at his gut. He wanted to tear the uniform off and burn it to ash, but he couldn't, not yet, and that made him feel like he was trapped in an SS prison once again.

"Go to sleep, Amos," he commanded, lying down and squeezing his eyes shut.

"All right...good night," the fugitive muttered, and a grunt was Samuel's only response. Black Fox 120 would be glad to be rid of Amos Auman.

Three

"This is it?"

"This is it."

"It's…not what I was expecting."

It wasn't what Samuel had been expecting either. Black Fox 120 had been ready for almost anything, but even he, well-experienced in the diverse array of men and women who joined the Black Foxes, lifted a curious brow and checked the map thrice before he conceded that they were in the right place.

Black Fox 10's safehouse was a villa surrounded by an ornate wrought-iron fence. It boasted a yard filled with toys, a tidy garden of white flowers that a twelve-year-old girl was tending to, and a flagpole that bore two banners: a red swastika flag and a black banner with the double lighting-bolt insignia of the SS.

"Is Black Fox Ten in the SS?" muttered Amos, a lilt of hope entering his voice as he peeked his head a bit too far out of the bushes across the street from the Nazi house where he and Black Fox 120 were hiding. Sam grunted and grabbed his charge's scarf, tugging once to remind Amos to keep his head down.

"I doubt it," Sam replied once Amos had retreated into the bushes again, touching the swastika armband on Franz's uniform and scowling at the Nazi flag fluttering proudly on Black Fox 10's property. "It's more likely that his wife is the Black Fox."

"Is that common?" Amos queried, sounding slightly disappointed, as though the existence of an SS man among the Black Foxes would have somehow made Franz Keidel a little less monstrous. Sam gritted his teeth.

"It wouldn't be the first time," the Russian said. The good German women and children of the Black Foxes who operated under their husbands' and fathers' noses were the veins of the Black Foxes, putting their lives in danger to right their wicked relatives' wrongs, acting as safehouses for the Jews on their way to neutral territory. Though Samuel despised Germany, the German Black Foxes' bravery and sacrifice kept him from praying that *Adonai* would decimate the entire nation like Sodom and Gomorrah.

"We need to approach with caution," Samuel declared. "There *is* a chance we were misled."

"You're wearing an SS uniform," Amos noted. "Can't you just walk up to the front door? Even if they're *not* Black Foxes…"

"You don't think they'd question a man with a Russian accent in a blood-splattered SS uniform?" Sam said, glancing at Amos and giving him the ghost of a snide smile. The fugitive cleared his throat and fiddled with his scarf.

"Ah…good point!" Amos conceded with an embarrassed chuckle. "So what do we do?"

Sam hummed thoughtfully and glanced at the twelve-year-old girl kneeling amongst the white flowers on the other side of the iron gate. The sun was beginning to dip over the horizon, and yet she was still at play, digging in the same spot over and over while humming...

"*Piano concerto number twenty-seven,*" Sam realized, almost letting a smirk flit across his face. "Very clever."

"What?" Amos muttered.

"Stay here," Sam commanded. Amos nodded and stayed crouching in the bushes while Sam stood and exited the thicket.

The manor was isolated, and there were no guards or soldiers manning the grounds, but nonetheless, Black Fox 120 scurried to the gate with the haste of a mouse skittering from its hole to snag a crumb.

The girl looked up as soon as she heard him, shoving her trowel into the dirt, standing, and striding to the gate. She was dressed in a checkered dress, her dark brown hair tied into two pigtails. Her girlish appearance was somewhat belied by the soldierly scowl that decorated her face as she examined the haggard Russian. Her clear blue eyes lingered on the stolen swastika armband before flitting to the blotches of Franz Keidel's blood decorating the Black Fox's breast.

"Pardon me, little one," Samuel said, doing his best to conceal his accent even though he was almost certain that the girl was an ally. "I've come to visit Papa, but I've brought no gift."

"That's all right, we have plenty of wine bottles," the girl said. Samuel nodded at the little Black Fox. Children and young teenagers were often some of their most effective agents: nobody would suspect them, particularly if they were the child of an SS officer.

Samuel waved for Amos to come out, and the fugitive scurried to Black Fox 120's side. Hastily, the twelve-year-old Black Fox opened the gate and ushered them inside the villa.

"Mama!" she cried as she slammed the door behind her and ran to close the blinds. "Visitors!"

Sam heard hurried footsteps upstairs. While he waited for Black Fox 10, he glanced about the SS home.

It was almost sickening how normal it appeared: toys and dolls strewn about the floor, too many blankets piled high on the couch, baskets of unfolded laundry resting here and there. His gut writhed as he was reminded of his home: the crowded, messy, humble Val household hadn't had nearly this much space, but there was still a familiar sort of coziness to this sort of chaos. The aura of a house occupied by untidy little girls.

A glance at the mantlepiece banished Samuel's nostalgia. While the Vals' fireplace had been decorated with a wax-coated menorah and letters that the Val children had written in Hebrew class, this mantle featured a shiny golden statue of an eagle clutching a swastika, plaques decorated with SS runes, and a painting of Adolf Hitler triumphantly lifting up a Nazi banner with the sun forming a halo about his head.

"Wow, I'm hideous!"

Amos' cheerful proclamation drew Sam's attention away from the Nazi adornments, and he almost snorted in amusement when he saw his charge. The fugitive had found an ornate mirror that hung beneath the staircase. He stood in front of his reflection, smiling and shaking his head as he drank in his shabby appearance: the forest hadn't been kind to Amos' wardrobe, which was covered in dirt, and the bit of stubble he'd accumulated didn't suit him.

Samuel realized right then that he hadn't beheld his own reflection since he had been captured by Franz Keidel's troop. The SS uniform he bore suddenly felt unduly heavy, and he leaned slightly forward to catch a glimpse at himself, morbidly wondering whether or not he looked like a convincing Nazi.

He let out a small sigh of relief when he saw himself: unshaven, covered in dried blood, bags weighing down his bright blue eyes. The rumpled uniform quite clearly wasn't his. Perhaps he should have been concerned that his disguise was utterly unconvincing, but it was a comfort right then.

"You look fine to me," a female voice said, weary and friendly at once. Sam and Amos both looked up at the staircase as a woman descended. Black Fox 10 seemed to be a typical *hausfrau*: she wore a long slightly rumpled dress with a checkered apron that matched her daughter's outfit. Her blonde hair was pulled into a tight bun. The heavy bags under her sapphire eyes made it clear that she was exhausted, either from wrangling her children or from wrangling fugitive Jews. Possibly both.

Around her neck was a golden necklace with a cross for a pendant. Once upon a time, Samuel might have regarded the Christian symbol with suspicion and disdain. Khruvina had been burned by those bearing the cross many times throughout her history, after all. His time in the Black Foxes had changed his view somewhat: most of the gentiles in the Black Foxes were devout Christians. He didn't share their faith, and he despised it when they tried to convince him to be baptized, but he appreciated their courage and sacrifice, nonetheless. If they were willing to put their lives in danger for men and women they saw as non-believers, he was willing to respect them even if, to him, the cross was little more than an idol.

"Black Fox Ten?" Sam queried with a polite nod. The woman nodded, fidgeting with the cross around her neck.

"And you've met Black Fox Twenty-Seven," Ten said, gesturing to her daughter. The twelve-year-old beamed as though merely hearing her code number filled her with pride.

"Sis is asleep?" Black Fox 27 asked, and Ten nodded.

"Just put her down," she said, looking up at Sam and explaining, "My youngest is five. Papa's little girl. Can't trust her to keep things secret."

"Understood," Sam said, dropping his voice lest he awaken the potential snitch. "I'm One-Twenty. Good to meet you."

"Ah, you work for One and Five, right? What are you doing all the way out here?" Ten queried, and her daughter must have been a heavy sleeper because she made no attempt to lower her own voice.

"Long story," Sam sighed, gesturing towards the bloody SS uniform. "I was on a personal mission, got captured, escaped, and now I have to get this man to safety."

He pointed to the fugitive at his side. Amos was staring longingly at the blanket-covered couch, but when he realized that Ten was looking at him, he offered her a bright smile.

"Hello! I'm Amos!" the fugitive declared, and Sam groaned and rubbed his forehead. Ten chuckled.

"Good to meet you, Amos," she said, offering a pristine palm and shaking the fugitive's dirty hand without pause.

"Don't say your name, stupid!" hissed Black Fox 27, scowling up at Amos, and Sam had to look away because her expression of irate disapproval was far too similar to the one Zofia had sported when she was reminded that girls couldn't be teachers in Khruvina no matter how hard they studied. Amos offered the twelve-year-old a smile and squatted down so that he was at eye level with her.

"Whoops! You're right, I'm definitely stupid!" he declared, smacking his own forehead. "You, on the other hand, you must be very smart to be such a high-ranked Black Fox! Twenty-Seven! You even outrank him."

Amos jabbed his thumb towards Sam, who grunted and rolled his eyes. Twenty-Seven's stony facade cracked, and she gave a small giggle, her eyes twinkling with childish joy.

"Twenty-Seven," Ten said in a tone that was at once maternal and commanding. "Why don't you take the guest upstairs? He looks like he could use a shave and a warm shower."

"Shower?" cried Amos, and now it was him that displayed childish glee. His turquoise eyes shimmered eagerly.

"Yeah, okay, c'mon. Be quiet, though: you don't wanna wake up my sister," Twenty-Seven said, grabbing Amos by the end of his turquoise scarf and giving the fabric an insistent tug.

"Be quick!" Ten commanded. "Then we'll get you a meal and get you to real safety."

Sam watched as Twenty-Seven led Amos up the staircase by his scarf like a dog on a leash. Amos didn't seem to mind the indignity; he all but skipped at her heels, eager to finally get clean. With a sigh, Samuel turned to Ten.

"Apologies, I couldn't get to a radio," he said. "Your daughter's smart, humming her designated song."

Black Fox Radio, which played classical music interspersed with American jazz, offered secret messages to Papa Fox's agents delivered via little ticks and bits of static in specific songs. The little girl had been clever enough to hum her particular song over and over, something that wouldn't arouse the suspicion of a passing SS troop but acted as a dead giveaway for her comrades. Ten smiled proudly and nodded.

"That was her idea. She takes after her father in some ways, but thankfully not others," Black Fox 10 mumbled, glancing mournfully at the swastika-clad mantle. "His cleverness but not his…ideology."

"That's good," Samuel said. He knew better than to ask any questions. The less he knew about the high-ranked Black Fox, the better.

"You two somehow managed to have both good and bad timing," Ten said. "My husband just called. He was in a meeting with Reinhard Heydrich…"

Heydrich. Merely hearing the name made the wound above Sam's heart burn. He couldn't possibly despise any man more than he despised Viktor Naden, but Reinhard Heydrich easily took second place. Heydrich was one of the Third Reich's most infamous monsters: Himmler's lackey, the Chief of the Gestapo, the ruler of occupied Czechoslovakia, and most pertinently for Samuel, Reinhard Heydrich was the man in charge of the *Einsatzgruppen*, the man who gave Viktor Naden his orders. Naden had been the one to strike the match that set Khruvina aflame, but he was ultimately a hitman in service of the so-called Man with the Iron Heart.

Samuel fully expected that any confrontation between himself and Viktor Naden would end in both of their deaths, but on the off chance he survived avenging Khruvina, he would immediately set his sights on Reinhard Heydrich. Make him face what he'd done. Make him pay.

But of course, his very first priority had to be Amos' safety. There would be plenty of time for hunting Heydrich and his cronies once the fugitive was out of his hair.

"I just need to contact my superiors," Sam said, fighting to maintain a neutral tone and banish all thoughts of the Man with the Iron Heart from his mind. "One or Five, either one, I just need to arrange for a meet-up close by."

"I can do that for you," Ten volunteered. "We can arrange for One to meet you by this old cafe a few miles from here. I'm sure she'll be happy to discover you're okay. Relatively sure you were written off for dead. I'm sure the story of your escape is…"

She gestured vaguely to Keidel's bloody SS uniform and let a smile bloom on her face. "Interesting."

"Very interesting," Sam concurred. "I'll tell you over a meal if you don't mind."

"A hot meal for you and your friend. But first let's make sure you're prepared for pick-up. You won't get far in *that* uniform."

Ten stepped close to Samuel, looking up and down thoughtfully. "You're about as tall as my husband," she observed. "And he doesn't do his own laundry."

"Doesn't look like *anyone* in this house does laundry," Sam said, remaining deadpan as he nodded towards the baskets of unfolded clothes. Ten snorted.

"Not you too," she muttered, gesturing for him to follow her up the stairs. "Come. I'll take that uniform off your hands and switch it out with a clean one. If I stitch up the holes, it'll be fine. My husband won't notice a few blood stains…"

Her voice trailed off and she spared a sorrowful glance at the fireplace, at her husband's awards, before clutching her cross pendant and starting up the staircase. Sam followed, but he remembered what Amos had said before about the uniform and heaved an aggravated, indulgent sigh..

"Would it be all right if I keep this uniform?" he said. Black Fox 10 stopped halfway up the stairs, turned, and regarded her comrade with a lifted brow.

"Long story," Samuel sighed, and the German woman shrugged.

"I doubt my husband would notice a missing uniform: as you observed, laundry isn't a big priority in this house. Nobody will buy that your friend is SS, but I suppose you could just shove it in your bag if you're desperate to keep it. Let's make sure you'll fit in one of my husband's uniforms. Take a shower after your friend is done. I'll contact Black Fox One."

"Will do," Sam said. The two Black Foxes tip-toed past a room decorated with pink paper hearts and puffy red letters that spelled out "*Heidi.*" Twenty-Seven bolted out of the room across from her sister's and greeted her comrades by pressing one finger to her lips and pointing towards Heidi's door.

"She's a deep sleeper, but hush anyways," the little Black Fox whispered, and Sam offered the girl a compliant nod.

"The civilian's showering?" Ten queried, and before her

daughter could answer, the telltale sound of pipes straining to feed a shower echoed about the house.

"Good," Ten said, gesturing towards Samuel. "Can you get our friends some supplies? Pack them a little bag in case they run into trouble. They'll be leaving before Papa gets home."

"I've got it," the girl agreed, clicking her muddy heels together like she truly was a soldier before darting down the stairs. Sam watched her with a heavy heart. She reminded him of Zofia: all too serious, determined to become a woman when she was still just a girl.

He shoved his hand into his pocket and gripped Naden's lighter, trying to suppress the memory of his sister as he followed Ten into the master bedroom.

"Feel free to lie down," Ten volunteered, waving towards the unmade bed as she ran to the walk-in closet. "You must be tired."

Sam didn't lie down or even sit, and though he tried not to glance about, knowing full well that a Black Fox was supposed to know as little about their comrades as possible, his eyes practically acted on their own. They flitted here and there, drinking in every detail of the Nazi's most private space.

This wasn't the first time he had encountered a Black Fox who was the wife of an SS man. To a certain extent, such agents had more protection than their comrades did, being above suspicion most of the time. On the other hand, however, they were always working right under the enemy's nose, and Adolf Hitler had trained the Germans to love him more than their own wives and mothers. Snitches and traitors were but a bedroom away for agents like Black Fox Ten, and once, Samuel had been acquainted with a woman who had suffered because of this. Anniska Engel. Black Fox 25.

Sam hadn't known Anniska terribly well, having only met her once or twice, but once upon a time she had been an important stop on the Black Foxes' underground railroad. When he and Black Fox Five had picked up Jewish children or families, they had previously dropped them off at Black Fox 25. Anniska had the ties and the resources to get those Jews false papers and then smuggle them to safety. She was, after all, married to Leon Engel, an SS man who was a prominent member of Hitler's personal bodyguard. She had been far above suspicion. Nobody would have ever thought that someone who paid visits to the Berghof, whose children had been hugged by Hitler himself, would be a member of the resistance.

But then her oldest son, Norman Engel, had discovered her Black Fox activities. And unlike Twenty-Seven, he hadn't joined his mother. The brainwashed teen had immediately called up the SS, sacrificing his own mother to the altar of Nazism. She had been arrested, and to prove that he was still a loyal Nazi, Leon Engel himself had shot his wife in the head. At the end of the day, Engel had decided that he loved Hitler more than Anniska. That decision had served him well: he was a national hero in the Reich, and his son was worshiped for his noble sacrifice.

Sam had often wondered if Anniska's husband had *ever* loved her, if she'd ever loved him, or if he'd been nothing more than a front and she'd been nothing but a baby factory for pumping out future Nazis. A relationship of pure convenience from both sides. He could only hope so, because he hated the idea that his comrade had been shot by someone she had actually loved.

Sam found himself wondering whether or not Black Fox 10 loved her husband, if she *could* love him knowing that he couldn't *truly* love her. Everyone in the Black Foxes knew what had happened to Anniska Engel, after all.

A brief glance about the room made it clear that she and her husband shared the space. (Unless the dresses that Black Fox 10 flung from the closet in her search for a suitable SS uniform were her husband's, which, given some of the rumors Sam had heard about Rudolf Hess and Hermann Goering, wasn't *entirely* out of the question.) A few pictures rested on a nearby dresser, pictures of what from a distance looked like a happy couple. He stepped close and grabbed one framed photo, lifting it up. A strangely casual image greeted him: Black Fox 10 clutching a baby to her chest, no doubt Heidi, while her husband held their eldest in his arms. Dressed in a sweater vest, slacks, and a fedora. Her husband was a handsome man with dark brown hair, striking blue eyes...

And a half-moon scar across his face.

Crack!

"All right, I found some—oh, dear."

Samuel didn't turn to look at Black Fox 10 as she emerged from the closet holding a fresh SS uniform, but he lifted his face to the vanity and stared at her surprised reflection. He had gripped the portrait so hard that the glass cracked.

"Your husband is Viktor Naden," he hissed. "The Beast of Belorussia."

Black Fox 10, the wife of the man who had burned little Cici Val to death, sighed heavily and tossed her husband's uniform onto the bed.

"Cat's out of the bag, then," she said, grasping her cross necklace. "I'm Katja Naden. Twenty-Seven is Nadine."

The scent of gasoline. Screams. The taste of ash on his tongue. The wound above his heart burned.

"You can't pretend that you don't know *exactly* what your husband does," Sam snarled. "How can you share a bed with that monster?"

Sam would have barely been willing to accept it if Katja proclaimed that she despised Viktor Naden, that the marriage was a sham maintained for the sake of smuggling Jews to safety.

But Katja instead wrapped her arms about herself and squeezed, staring mournfully at what must have been the Beast of Belorussia's side of the bed.

"I love Viktor, but he shames me," she confessed, glancing down at her glittering golden cross. "I think deep down he is a good man…"

Crack! Another break line appeared on the portrait.

"Good men don't do the things Viktor Naden does." Samuel could barely speak because his throat was so tight. He felt like he was choking on smoke.

"You're right," Katja concurred, her sorrow morphing into sternness as she looked away from her cross, at a Bible propped up on a nearby nightstand. "Even if he *could* have been a good man…he's made choices that are…"

She shivered, touching her cross. "I know that Christ can forgive any sin, but Viktor's only God is Hitler. I *tried* to make him see the truth, but he just won't *listen*, no matter what I say. 'Women shouldn't get involved in politics, they're too emotional,' he'd say. I *do* love him, but he's so entrenched in Nazism. I don't think there's a way to pull him out of it."

"No," Sam growled. "There isn't. You should have killed him in his sleep."

"I couldn't do that…" Katja whispered, her scowl dissipating, her eyes widening, her hands trembling as they both wrapped around her pendant. "Even if it's right, he's my husband, my children's father. I couldn't kill him. Besides, I can do more good like this, saving people under his nose. He'll get justice someday, from God or someone else. But not me."

"Yes…" Sam muttered, setting the picture face-down on the dresser. "Yes, he will."

"I'll leave the uniform here," Katja said, giving the back of her comrade's head a soft smile and gesturing to the grey uniform that lay on Viktor Naden's side of the bed. "Shower and come down for a meal. I'll send word to Black Fox One while you do so."

Sam barely saw her leave as his vision turned red, flaming red. His pulse pounded in his ears. The wound above his heart was consuming his whole body. The lighter in his pocket felt heavy. He drew it from the depths and flicked it on, looking at the soft glow of the miniscule flame.

"An eye for an eye," Samuel whispered, and his heart became rigid as iron.

"Oh, One-Twenty! Black Fox Ten says she doesn't have anything kosher."

"Nothing kosher *butchered*, but there's no dairy or pork, just lamb. I figure God won't mind in this situation."

"I'm not picky on missions," Sam said as he strode into

the kitchen. Katja was giving a freshly shaved and showered Amos Auman a bowl of some sort of meat stew. She quickly took in her comrade's appearance and gave a nod of approval.

"Good, the uniform fits you," Katja said. Amos' gaze flitted to Sam's uniform, and the fugitive's shoulders stiffened when he realized that Black Fox 120 had shorn Franz Keidel's garments. The newly clean-shaven Russian wore a fresh, slightly rumpled ash-grey outfit, the uniform of Viktor Naden. He'd even donned an SS cap and polished jackboots.

"I'll be a convincing SS man?" Sam said, taking a seat beside Amos and watching the fugitive squirm out of the corner of his eye.

"From a distance, just don't open your mouth," Katja advised, giving the Russian a bowl of soup. He finished it even though his gut was roiling. Amos somehow downed a third bowl—it was a wonder he was so small if he could eat like that.

"Where's Twenty-Seven?" Sam asked as he and Amos handed Katja their empty dishes.

"Basement," she answered, gesturing towards a door in the other room. "Packing you some supplies. We're not very neat in this house, so she had trouble finding a canteen. She'll be finished in a moment. Black Fox One will be sending Fifty-Six. You know the code."

"Right. What time?"

"Thirty minutes."

"Enough time for a drink, then. Have any vodka?"

"You think it's a good idea to drink on a mission?" Katja said, her voice becoming teasingly maternal.

"I'm Russian, I'll be fine," Sam assured her, letting the

corner of his lip curl slightly. Amos and Katja both chuckled.

"All right," Katja said. "But just a little to soothe your nerves."

Sam watched as she reached into one particular cabinet, pulled out a vodka bottle, poured him a shot, and put it back. He downed it quickly, earning a low whistle from Amos.

"Wow. I think I'd die if I did that." Amos chuckled. "Could barely keep down a mug of beer."

"Germans are weaklings," Sam said, turning his small glass upside-down on the table. "Ten, will you excuse us? I want to have a chat with Amos before we go."

"A chat about…?" she said.

"Personal matter. Mutual friend," Sam explained brusquely, glancing at Amos, whose eyes shimmered. Their only mutual "friend" was Franz Keidel.

"All right," Katja sighed. "We'll be ready to go in a moment. Don't be long."

"We won't. C'mon, Amos."

Eagerly, Amos followed Black Fox 120 up the stairs, his enthusiastic stride only faltering when they passed Heidi's room and Sam urged him to be quiet lest they wake the child.

"Here," Sam said, opening the door to Viktor and Katja's room. Amos might have noticed that the blanket and sheets had been stripped off the bed, but he was too distracted by a folded-up blood-smattered uniform sitting in the midst of the barren mattress.

"Oh! It's Franz's uniform!" Amos cried happily, running to the bed and picking it up. "I hope those stains can come…*unk*!"

But before Amos could get out another word, Sam struck him on the back of the head with the butt of his stolen Luger. The blow was enough to stun Amos, making him collapse on top of the bed and giving Sam an opportunity to tie the smaller man's wrists behind his back using some of the makeshift rope he had fashioned from the Nadens' bedding.

"W-wait…" Amos gasped, and his entire body went rigid. He craned his neck back and regarded Black Fox 120 with a haunted look in his turquoise eyes. Something about that terrified expression made Sam's resolve falter, and he leapt away from the tied-up man.

"W-what are you doing?" Amos said, his voice barely a rasp. It seemed like he was about to have a heart attack.

"Sorry," Sam said, trying for a comforting tone, attempting to assure Amos that he didn't intend on making him into collateral damage. "I'll get you to safety later, but I can't let you get in my way."

Amos exhaled, and his body relaxed a tad. Whatever he had feared that Sam was going to do to him, it appeared he now knew it wouldn't be happening.

"In your way of what?" Amos asked, now sounding more curious than frightened, rolling so that he wasn't face-down in Franz's dried blood. Sam gestured to the fresh uniform he wore.

"Ten's husband is the Beast of Belorussia," he explained. "Have you heard of him?"

"No."

"He destroyed my village. Killed my sisters, my parents, everyone I knew," Sam hissed, and it felt strangely liberating to say that aloud. He had never talked about what had happened to Khruvina, what had happened to *him*. A part of him wanted to sob, but there was no room for sorrow in his soul right then. Only anger.

"You're going to kill him when he gets home," Amos realized, and there was a note of approval in his voice. "All right, but what about Ten and Twenty-Seven? Won't that harm their cover? Are you gonna tie them up too?"

Sam said nothing, but the blaze in his eyes spoke for him. Amos' jaw dropped.

"No," the helpless man gasped, shaking his head. "No, no, *One-Twenty!*"

"*Ain takhat ain.* An eye for an eye," Sam declared, turning on his heel and strutting out of the Beast of Belorussia's room.

"One-Twenty!" Amos screamed, and if Samuel had been able to think clearly right then, if the flame in his heart weren't all-consuming, he might have hesitated because his fellow Jew's tone was familiar: one of utter terror. "*One-Twenty!* Don't do this! Don't hurt–!"

But Sam slammed the door shut, leaving Amos to writhe about in a desperate attempt to escape.

"Is everyone all right? I thought I heard…" Katja Naden had barely made it halfway up the stairs when she found herself facing the barrel of a Luger.

"Hands up," Sam commanded, his hypnotic blue eyes blazing in a frighteningly familiar way. She obeyed.

"W-What are you doing?" she asked as he led her downstairs and commanded her to sit in a kitchen chair. He didn't answer, silently tying her up with what appeared to be her own bedsheets.

"One-Twenty, we're comrades! Hey—!" Katja cried, but she was silenced as he gagged her with a piece of blanket and blinded her with another rag.

Wordlessly, Sam went into the basement to retrieve Nadine, refusing to glance at the mirror as he moved.

"SHIT, SHIT, *SHIT!* DAMN IT!"

Amos Auman had skinny wrists, which in the past, when he'd been hog-tied in the forest and left for dead, had been a blessing. Back then, he'd been able to wriggle out of his bonds and run to relative safety. Unfortunately, either Franz Keidel's care had led to him gaining weight, or Black Fox 120 was simply better at tying knots than the Kommandant that had used him, abused him, and then left him to starve in the woods.

Amos heard a little girl shriek. Panic erupted in his belly.

"Okay…okay…" he panted, pressing his cheek against the uniform of Franz Keidel. "Damn…damn, come on, *think*…oh, Franz, what would you…?"

Realization struck him. *Franz!* Amos squirmed again and realized that an old gift from his SS beau was still buried deep in one of his pockets: a pocketknife. Franz had given it to Amos in case he ever needed to protect himself, and now it was little Heidi Naden's only hope.

Amos wriggled and wriggled, and the knife inched towards the mouth of his pocket. A small part of him recognized that even if he managed to escape, he couldn't hope to physically stop Black Fox 120. Amos could barely use a knife, and the Black Fox had a gun.

Even if Amos had himself possessed a firearm, he wasn't sure he'd be willing to use it. Black Fox 120 was horribly wrong, but Amos knew exactly what he was feeling. When the Nazis had butchered his own family, Amos had embraced despair. Black Fox 120, meanwhile, had wrapped a comforting shield of anger about himself. It was understandable after what he had been through. Amos would have been lying if he'd declared that he had never fantasized about making the man that had killed his family suffer.

Another shriek. Amos snarled.

He still has to be stopped! He's going too far, thought Amos, writhing frantically until the knife finally slipped out of his pocket and unto the mattress.

"Yes!" he hissed. "Thank you, Franz!"

He rolled over and grabbed the knife with his tied-up hands, unsheathing the blade and praying that he wouldn't be too late.

Four

Viktor Naden was happy to be home. *Really* home.

Being back in Germany was a blessing and a curse. On one hand, it was good to be in a civilized country. Good to take a break from the gore and violence, from the tiny villages full of stinking Jews and barbaric Slavs. It was good to wear a crisp, clean uniform that wasn't covered in ash. It was good to hear the shrieks of children at play instead of children burning to death…

On the other hand, whenever he returned to the *Altreich*, he wasn't given much time to actually enjoy it. He was usually on-call even when he was far away from the front, obligated to meet with underlings and superiors alike.

Worst of all, he had to report to Reinhard Heydrich, his Chief, a thoroughly unpleasant icicle of a human being who was despised by ally and enemy alike. Viktor would rather be left unarmed in a village full of Jewish Black Foxes than spend more than ten minutes in the presence of Reinhard Heydrich.

Thankfully, he'd finally managed to escape the Man

with the Iron Heart and journey home. Viktor hadn't seen his daughters or his wife in too long, and he was determined to make the little time they would have together before he went back to the Eastern Front pleasant.

He pulled up to his house and glanced at the gifts he'd brought, which sat in a pile on the passenger's seat. For his wife, a dozen red roses and a pearl necklace. For studious little Nadine, a book about Julius Caesar. For precious little Heidi, a pink toy bunny rabbit with a purple bow wrapped around its neck.

I hope this is enough, Viktor thought, making sure his hair was tidy and gathering the presents into his arms. *I've been away too long. They deserve more...should have gotten them those bracelets.*

Viktor glanced at Nadine's little garden as he exited his car and marched up the path to his front door, smiling when he saw Heidi's dolls strewn about the yard. He had missed Heidi's birthday this year, and though he'd showered her in gifts and love when he'd returned and she hadn't seemed to mind, it still felt awful. Like a part of his soul was being stolen.

She's very little....Nadine must be even more upset, seeing so little of me. And poor Katja! If she cheated on me with the postman, I wouldn't even blame her at this point.

Ruminating on the memories and time he had lost made a fire of anger erupt in his chest. Anger at an enemy that existed only to cause misery, anger at the creatures who kept stealing him from his family: the Jews. If they didn't exist, if they weren't so awful, if they didn't *need* to be exterminated, then he wouldn't have *had* to be in the SS. He wouldn't have *had* to go into Russia and burn them like plague-ridden rats.

He shook his head. *It will be over soon,* he assured himself. *The Final Solution will be completed, and then you'll have more time with your girls. You can spoil them then, when they're completely safe, and they can brag to all their friends about what you did. For now, just enjoy what you have.*

With that thought, Viktor banished fury to the back of his mind and inhaled deeply, letting a smile conquer his scarred face as he entered the house.

"Girls!" he cried cheerfully. "Papa's home! I've got—!"

Viktor had been expecting to find the girls awake long past their bedtime, sitting in the living room and waiting to run and greet him.

But instead he entered his home and found himself facing a man in a rumpled SS uniform, a man with eyes identical to those of the Führer. Bright blue and blazing with hatred.

The strange man with the frighteningly hypnotic blue eyes was standing in the middle of the entrance hall. Katja, Nadine, and Heidi were tied to chairs and blindfolded. Nadine and Katja had been gagged, but Heidi's mouth was uncovered. The little girl, still in her pink nightgown, sobbed wildly.

"Papa!" Heidi squeaked, but the stranger pressed the barrel of a Luger to her temple. Confusion and terror clashed in Viktor's heart. An SS man in his home, threatening his family? Had he angered someone? Had Heydrich decided to get rid of him?

The stranger spoke: "Hands up."

His accent gave him away. Not an SS man, a Russian. Katja must have let him into the house, assuming he was a comrade. Viktor gritted his teeth and dropped the gifts, lifting up his hands.

"Toss your gun over there," the Russian commanded, nudging his head towards the living room and jabbing the barrel of his gun at Heidi's skull. "No funny business. I don't need all three of them."

"Okay," Viktor agreed, struggling to maintain a calm, almost friendly tone even as he felt like his heart was about to break through his chest. He slowly grabbed his gun with two fingers, lifting it from its holster and letting it dangle from his weak grasp. "See? Okay…"

Viktor tossed the gun away and raised up his hands again.

"There, see?" the Nazi Captain said. "I'll cooperate. You can take me as your prisoner."

"Kneel down. Hands behind your head. No sudden movements or I'll blow the girl's head off," the Russian warned. Katja let out a muffled whimper. Nadine writhed. Heidi bawled.

"Papa, Papa!" the five-year-old yelped. "I'm scared!"

"It's all right, *liebchen*," Viktor said gently, obeying the Russian's command. His pounding heart calmed ever so slightly when the Russian stepped away from Heidi and strode behind the *Einsatzgruppen* Captain, trampling on the biography of Julius Caesar as he clapped a pair of handcuffs on Viktor's wrists. Good, it seemed the Russian didn't intend on causing any collateral damage; his aim was merely to catch the infamous Beast of Belorussia. Viktor would probably be stolen away, tortured for information, and then beaten to death.

Fine, Viktor thought, gazing at his helpless family and trying to find the proper words to say goodbye. He had always been willing to die for the Reich. As long as they were safe…

Before he could submit to his captor and think of what his last words would be—either "Heil Hitler!" or "Long live Germany!"—the Russian dragged him not out the front door, but towards the staircase.

"W-what are you doing?" Viktor stuttered as the Russian took a rope fashioned from torn-up bedsheets and tied the handcuffed Einsatzgruppen Captain to the stair rail, forcing him to kneel on the floor and face his tied-up family. With Viktor Naden rendered an utterly helpless audience, the Russian stood above him and tiled his SS visor cap back, revealing more of his young face.

"Do you recognize me?" the Russian asked, his tone cold and vicious. It reminded Naden of Heydrich in the worst way. The Einsatzgruppen Captain was afraid to be honest, but he had no choice.

"N-No...*unk!*"

The Russian kicked him in the stomach. Pain erupted in Viktor's chest. He felt his ribcage crack as his own lead-lined jackboot struck him, and he coughed up a wad of blood.

"Papa! Papa, are you okay?" Heidi cried.

"I'm fine, *liebchen!*" Viktor assured her even though saying even a single word was agonizing. He may have been a frontline soldier, but he targeted civilians, women and children and old men all unarmed and too terrified to even think of fighting back. He hadn't actually fought in years, and he hadn't had a beating since SS training camp.

The Russian growled and brought one jackboot down on Viktor's crotch, making the Nazi cry out in agony despite his best attempt to keep quiet lest he frighten his poor daughter. That pain was particularly intense, and it took a few moments for Viktor to recover enough to look up once more. The Russian leaned down, nearly nose-to-nose with the Beast of Belorussia.

"Fine," he spat. "Then do you recognize this?"

The Russian reached into his pocket and pulled out something small and gold, holding it right up to Viktor's face. The Nazi Captain's vision was blurry from pain, but he blinked and managed to see what it was: a familiar golden trinket engraved with his name. *V. Naden.*

"My lighter," Viktor mumbled. "I dropped it…"

"In the village of Khruvina." The Russian reached up, undid the top buttons of his stolen SS uniform, and pulled it down, ripping it slightly as he revealed a barely healed wound just above his heart.

Any amount of hope in Viktor's soul died right then as he realized what the intruder was. Not merely a barbaric Russian. A soulless Jew. The Devil in human form.

SAMUEL HAD FANTASIZED ABOUT HIS VENGEANCE ALMOST every minute of every day since the end of his old life, but he hadn't imagined that when it happened it would feel this good. To see a demon brought to his knees. To see that moon-scarred face turn pale with horror when he realized what was going to happen to him. Viktor Naden had once been a cold-eyed God of Death, but now the tables had turned. Now Samuel Val, sole survivor of the Khruvina massacre, had the power to destroy him.

It felt good. Good in the same way that it had felt good when he was young and had brought his boot down on a spider that frightened his sister. He felt powerful, but more than that, the sense of power was matched by a righteous fire, by the knowledge that the pitiful beast he crushed *deserved* its fate. Viktor Naden *deserved* his punishment. Sam was a vessel of divine judgment, the Angel of Death striking Pharaoh's heart.

"You burned my village to the ground," Samuel declared, his voice booming, making the Nazi wince like the sinners of Nineveh confronted with a warning from a prophet. "You killed my family, everyone I loved! You *burned my sisters to death!*"

He kicked Naden again. The yelp of pain he earned from the butcher made his heart soar. Heidi Naden cried and screamed and begged him not to hurt her papa, and while a small part of Samuel's soul begged him to have empathy for the little girl that had done nothing wrong, the anger burning him inside out made it all intoxicating. Heidi screamed, and she deserved it because she was Naden's, and Naden *deserved* to watch her suffer.

Naden took a moment to recover, and curiously enough, he didn't immediately look at Samuel when he stopped grimacing in pain. Rather, his bright blue eyes flitted towards Katja, who was sitting stiff as a board. The Nazi Captain's cheeks flushed, and Samuel was surprised to see a flicker of embarrassment flash across his scarred face. Not quite *shame*, because *shame* would have meant that he knew what he did was wrong, but *embarrassment*, no doubt because his wife had known that he killed Jewish children but hadn't known *how* he killed them.

"Yes, I burned your village, I remember," Naden stuttered, and he sounded hoarse, as though confessing the full truth in front of his wife and daughters was physically painful. The Beast of Belorussia looked away from his family and met Samuel's frosty gaze. "So you're going to burn me, right?"

Naden's voice, once cold and commanding, was now frenzied. It sounded almost like he was pleading for Sam to say *yes.*

"No," Sam hissed. "No, you deserve much worse."

Samuel turned on his heel, pausing to stomp on the bouquet of roses Naden had brought, then kicking the little pink rabbit toy under the couch before he strode towards Heidi. The *thud, thud, thud* of his jackboots striking the dusty floor echoed about the house.

"What are you doing?" Naden asked, anger and terror melding in his voice. "*What* are you doing?!"

"This one…" Sam grabbed one of Heidi's golden pigtails and gave it a harsh tug. The girl let out a shriek.

"Ow! Ow, that hurt! Papa!" she howled, but her plea was only rewarded with another vicious pull on her hair. Her scream was an echo of Cici's, and watching Naden writhe and fight his bonds, helpless to save his daughter, made Sam's iron heart swell.

"Stop it!" Viktor demanded.

"She's papa's little girl, hm?" Sam hissed. "She's five, right? My sister was only seven when you killed her."

Another tug, another scream from Heidi.

"*Stop it!*" Now Viktor Naden was no longer commanding like an SS man but pleading like a desperate father. "Stop it, don't hurt her!"

"Papa, Papa!" the girl shrieked. Katja and Nadine squirmed, but Sam ignored them. His eyes were fixed on Viktor Naden, busily etching the Beast of Belorussia's expression of defeated agony into his memory. Black Fox 120 smiled as he walked out of the room.

"What are you doing?" Naden cried. Samuel snatched the vodka from the cabinet Katja had unwittingly shown him earlier and returned to the entrance hall. He unscrewed the cap, tossed it aside, and took a hearty swig.

"What did your men drink? They all smelled like booze when they were invading Khruvina," Sam asked. He strutted back to Heidi and held the still mostly full bottle under her nose. The girl whimpered and squirmed.

"What are you doing?" Viktor asked again, now barely able to choke.

Sam's smile vanished. His expression became steely, soulless. Just like Viktor Naden's that morning in Khruvina.

"*Ain takhat ain.* An eye for an eye," the Jew hissed, turning the bottle upside down and dumping its contents all over Heidi. The girl sputtered and gasped.

"Ow, ow, it stings, Papa!" Heidi shrieked. "It stings, ow!"

Realization came to Viktor Naden's blue eyes, and he howled, writhing and yanking on his bonds in a futile attempt to escape. The Beast of Belorussia was sobbing now, tears tracing his moon-shaped scar.

"Stop, stop, please, stop!" Naden begged. "I'm sorry, I'm so sorry!"

Fury consumed Samuel's soul. He brought the bottle down on the back of Heidi's chair. It shattered. Heidi screamed as shards of glass sunk into her exposed flesh and clung to her hair.

"No, you're not!" Sam barked, tossing the broken bottle aside and striking the girl on the back of the head to emphasize his anger. "No, you're fucking not!"

Samuel ignored Heidi's howls, didn't look at the blood gushing from the wounds he'd given her, didn't think about the time Cici had stepped on a shard of broken glass and how furious he'd been with himself for dropping a cup and not cleaning up thoroughly. He didn't think about that, he *couldn't*, because he was too busy staring at the bawling Beast of Belorussia. Slowly, Samuel reached into his pocket and pulled out the lighter.

"And even if you were," he said, flicking his finger and creating a weak little flame. "I don't give a shit."

He savored the moment of absolute power as he held the lighter above the screaming little girl. One little movement of his fingers and the flame would drop. The tiniest motion would destroy Viktor Naden. The power of more than just life and death, but the soul. Fury melded with *that feeling*, that righteous, Godlike feeling, and he watched, unsure if he felt enraged or satisfied as Naden realized that he couldn't escape and resorted to begging.

"Please, please, don't hurt her!" the Nazi pleaded, barely able to get the words out through sobs. "Please, don't hurt my little girl, please, *please!*"

"Why?" The question fell from Sam's lips, cold as a Russian winter. Naden's light blue eyes were round. He let out a small, confused noise.

"Why? Give me one reason," Sam demanded, lowering his hand, bringing the flame slightly closer to the alcohol-covered child. "Give me one good reason *not* to do it. *One.*"

The Beast of Belorussia choked, regarding the imperious intruder with a look of resigned horror as he realized that he couldn't answer. His own worldview decreed that Samuel Val had no reason to spare Heidi Naden.

The Beast of Belorussia kept begging for mercy even though he was sure that it wouldn't work, and Sam savored every sob, every helpless plea.

"One-Twenty!"

A different voice, a familiar voice. It made the God-like feeling falter.

Amos Auman bolted halfway down the stairs before he froze, gripping the rail and drinking in the awful scene. The makeshift rope restraints, half cut, still hung from Amos' wrists and he clutched a pocketknife that Sam hadn't known he'd been carrying.

That feeling, that divine feeling of being in command, returned when Sam saw realization clash with horror in Amos' turquoise eyes. He was already too late. He could do nothing. One wrong move and Sam would simply drop the flame.

The fugitive Jew and Black Fox 120 stared at one another, Sam's eyes blazing with agonized delight, Amos' gaze flitting from the wailing little girl to the frantic Nazi Captain.

But then Amos' wide eyes narrowed, and a chastising flare came to his turquoise irises identical to the sort that had flashed in Yonatan's eyes once upon a time. The sort that had always subdued Samuel when he misbehaved.

"Look at yourself!" Amos cried, pointing downwards. "One-Twenty, look at yourself!"

Sam's eyes followed Amos' finger to the ornate mirror that hung beneath the staircase.

Where once there had been a ragged resistance fighter in disguise, now there was a monster. Clean-shaven with a slightly rumpled SS uniform grey as the ash of Khruvina's synagogue. Dark hair, bright blue eyes. If he only had a scar, Samuel Val would have looked just like Viktor Naden.

The feeling of power, of God-like strength, faded into

nausea. Samuel looked at the lighter in his hand and then glanced at his reflection.

A little girl screaming, the heavy scent of booze, and a monster with a golden lighter. The wound above his heart burned worse than it ever had.

He extinguished the flame and threw the lighter away. It landed by Naden's knees. The Beast of Belorussia watched with disbelief and horror as Sam stumbled away from Heidi, looking down at his own quaking hands, guilt flowing from his eyes.

"I...I..." Sam gasped, staring at the black gloves covering his hands, tears escaping his bright blue eyes. It felt like the part of his soul he had buried in fury had broken free of its bonds, and now it berated him. One little movement, one moment of weakness, and he would have…

What were you thinking? Sam's conscience screamed. *What were you thinking?!*

He barely heard Amos' footsteps as the fugitive ran down the stairs and grabbed his wrists.

"Hey!" Amos cried, and Sam's head snapped up. Amos' eyes glistened with pride and desperation.

"Let's go," he begged. "Let's just go, let's go…"

All thoughts of vengeance long gone. Deep, horrific disgust consumed Samuel as he nodded. It may have been good, ultimately, if he had put a bullet between the Nazi Captain's eyes right then, but for once Samuel Val couldn't think of Viktor Naden. He just wanted to run, run and get away from the sobbing girl, the comrade he'd betrayed, this damned house that smelled of vodka, and his own reflection.

Samuel bolted out the door, running right past the Beast

of Belorussia. Amos only spared one second to cut Katja Naden's bonds before he hastily followed Black Fox 120.

"One-Twenty, wait up!" Amos cried as he dashed away from the Nadens' villa, nearly tripping over the toys Heidi had left strewn about the yard as he followed Sam into the dark.

Sam didn't slow down, however. He ran into the woods, ran and ran until it felt like his every sinew was on fire. He ran until his legs gave out and he collapsed into the mud, gasping and panting, trying to cool his boiling lungs.

"W-wait…" Almost miraculously, Amos managed to keep up with the Black Fox. The strangely swift fugitive recovered from his sprint quickly, sucking a deep breath and offering Sam a hand.

"Are you okay?" Amos asked when the Russian didn't even look up. Sam remained on his hands and knees, sobbing, gasping for air, and muttering prayers in Hebrew, the prayers his father had taught him to recite when he sinned. *God can forgive **almost** anything,* Yonatan had once said with a chuckle, because he certainly would have never thought that sweet, faithful Samuel would ever come close to committing one of the few unforgivable sins.

"Hey, hey, come on, I can't understand you! Are you okay?" Amos knelt before the Black Fox, reaching out and grasping his shoulders. Sam looked up, his eyes round and filled with tears.

"Come on, breathe, breathe!" Amos urged gently. "You didn't do anything, she's fine, you stopped, you stopped…"

"I stopped…" Sam gasped. "I was…I was so angry…I felt…it felt…"

He couldn't begin to describe it. *That feeling.* That temptingly toxic blend of anger and powerful delight, that sensation of being a God stomping on sinful little ants. To have that sort of power and to feel justified, *obliged*, to use it against a creature that deserved whatever it got. *That feeling* which told him that it didn't matter how cruel he became. It was fine. It was *right*.

There was no doubt that Viktor Naden had been utterly consumed by *that feeling* when he'd burned Khruvina to the ground.

"It's okay," Amos assured Samuel, patting his shoulders the way his mother had when he was very little and would break something that was easily fixed or replaced. "It's okay…"

"It *isn't*," Sam said, wiping his face with one grimy hand and leaving a streak of mud on his cheek. When he realized he was still wearing Viktor Naden's black gloves, Viktor Naden's torn SS uniform, he shivered. It felt like cock-roaches were crawling all over him. He tore off the gloves, the tunic. He was almost tempted to rip off the trousers, but he resisted. It wouldn't do to be wandering around the Reich without pants.

That thought made a small smile tug at his lip, and despite himself, Samuel let out a gasp that was half a laugh, half a sob. Amos, seemingly possessed by a strange spirit of post-traumatic levity, chuckled a bit.

"You really scared me," Amos said. "You pulled your-self out of it, though. You should be proud."

Proud. Samuel was anything but *proud*. It felt like an inky hand had grasped his soul, and though he'd wrenched himself from its grasp, the stains remained.

"I almost did it, I *almost*, I was *this* close before…"

This close, too close, and yet the man he had been so eager to get rid of because he was too soft, too optimistic, had saved both Heidi and Samuel. If Amos hadn't been there, then Heidi would have burned, and Samuel would have forfeited his soul to vengeance. The Russian grabbed Amos' hand and squeezed it fraternally. "Thank you, thank you…I owe you…"

"Hey, hey, you don't owe me anything. *You* made a choice, not me," Amos interrupted, patting Black Fox 120's forearm. "You made the right choice, and you didn't even need a whale to swallow you."

Amos smiled devilishly and Sam, unable to stop himself, broke, laughing in a manner he hadn't since Viktor Naden had burned Khruvina. He shoved Amos playfully, the way he used to push Cici when she picked her nose and wiped it on him, sending the fugitive falling into the mud. Amos cackled, pushing him right back.

When the two men finally stopped laughing, they were both covered in mud, red-faced, and grinning. Though Samuel still felt guilt weighing down his soul, the rest of him felt strangely light, and he managed to easily hop to his feet.

"Come on," he said. "Let's hurry to the rendezvous point."

Amos stood up and jabbed his thumb back in the direction of the Nadens' villa. "You don't think Black Fox Ten will…?"

"No. I doubt it," Samuel answered, shaking his head. "She wouldn't want to punish you for what I did."

"What you *didn't* do, you mean," Amos pointed out. "All right. You think we'll make it without…?"

Amos nudged Naden's torn-up uniform with his toe. Sam nodded.

"Yeah, yeah, we'll make it," he declared, and he had

never been so glad that he was certain he wouldn't be joining his family in Heaven anytime soon.

"All right," Amos declared, throwing the end of his turquoise scarf over his shoulder. "Then let's hurry, One-Twenty…"

"Sam."

Amos tilted his head to the side. Sam offered the fugitive a hand.

"It's Sam," he said. "You deserve to know. I trust you."

"Sam…" Amos repeated, beaming as he shook his friend's hand. "Good to meet you, Sam!"

HEIDI WAS SAFE. SHAKEN, BRUISED, NURSING A FEW CUTS from the broken bottle, but perhaps in time she would regard all of this as nothing more than a bad dream.

Nadine was safe, and strangely unaffected, seemingly more *annoyed* than traumatized as she led her freshly bandaged sister up the stairs and back to bed.

Katja was safe. Anxious, confused, and relieved all at once. She was safe, and her family was safe despite everything. She shepherded her girls upstairs and then came down to speak to her husband, whom she had freed from his handcuffs with a lockpick. Viktor was sitting on the bottom step, cradling the little golden lighter that the intruder had abandoned in his palm.

"Viktor…?" Katja mumbled, slowly trotting down the stairs and standing before him. She could barely believe it when she saw her husband's face. Viktor Naden wore an expression she would have never imagined he would ever don: an expression of utter confusion.

"It doesn't make sense," Viktor mumbled, staring down at his own gold-engraved name. "It doesn't make sense…"

"Vik, my love?" Katja stepped forward, ready to put a hand on his shoulder.

"Why *didn't* he do it? Why?" Viktor whispered, his voice hoarse, fear blooming in his eyes even though the threat was long gone. Katja retracted her hand, clutching the cross around her neck.

"Vik?" she whispered.

"They're supposed to be soulless…they're not supposed to…he didn't have a reason to…not after I…" Viktor closed a trembling hand around the lighter.

"They're supposed to be evil, that's why, that's why we *have* to…"

Naden's eyes flitted to the awards hanging above the mantle, awards he had earned by burning Jewish villages, butchering little Jewish children, killing the family of the supposedly devilish Jewish man that had nonetheless offered *his* family mercy.

"Why *didn't* he do it?" Viktor repeated. He looked up at his wife, and Katja wasn't sure if she should feel hope or horror when she saw the utterly lost look in his eyes.

"I don't understand," the Beast of Belorussia whimpered. "I don't understand…"

Epilogue

A few days had passed since the incident with Black Fox 120. Viktor had gone back to work. He hadn't wanted to so soon after the traumatizing incident with the Russian Black Fox, after he had nearly lost his two girls. He hadn't wanted to leave while Heidi was begging him to stay and protect her from any more "bad guys."

But although Viktor had told his boss what had happened and begged for a few days off to recover with his daughters, Reinhard Heydrich had been completely unsympathetic. That was to be expected. The Man with the Iron Heart was eternally unkind and unmerciful even towards his most loyal underlings.

And so Viktor had set off, leaving Katja to reassure little Heidi that there would be no more bad guys, that nothing would hurt her. Nadine was a great help, stoic and bold as she was in the face of everything. Katja herself was struggling to conceal her own lingering anxiety. She still shivered when she recalled the smell of vodka, the rogue Black Fox's threats against her daughter, his *eyes*…

Katja still hadn't reported Black Fox 120 to any of her superiors yet. She hadn't gotten the opportunity since Viktor had only been gone for a day and Heidi could barely tolerate being left by herself. Nevertheless, Katja wasn't sure if she would report him when she could. On one hand, he had threatened her precious daughters. On the other hand, her husband had undoubtedly deserved it. *You burned my sisters to death,* the Russian had said. She had known that her husband was a monster, but she hadn't known just how thoroughly evil he had become.

No, she couldn't blame Black Fox 120 for his over-whelming rage. And he had stopped, spared her children, spared even her horrible husband. His entire stunt hadn't even led to her and Nadine being unmasked as Black Foxes. Christ would have wanted her to forgive him, and so she would have to try.

After a few days, Heidi began to tolerate being watched by her sister instead of her mother, and Katja decided it was time to continue her duties. She readied herself to contact her superiors and request another transport, having no intention of mentioning what her comrade had almost done.

Barely had she decided that she was prepared to serve the Black Foxes again when there was a knock at the door.

Who could that be? Katja wondered, skittering through the entrance hall and pausing to tidy herself in the mirror before she opened the door.

"Heil Hitler, madam!" chirped the man standing on her porch. It was a young SS officer: shorter than her husband with sandy blonde hair, lapis-colored eyes, and handsome, familiar features. Was he a propaganda poster boy? Katja knew that she had seen him before, but she couldn't recall *where.*

The guest lifted up his hand to give the Nazi salute, and Katja saw a patch on his arm: "SD." The *Sicherheitsdienst*, the intelligence arm of the SS. This was one of Heydrich's men.

"Heil Hitler," Katja said, lifting up her hand and flashing him a smile, fighting to keep herself from nervously fidgeting with her cross necklace. She scrutinized the SD officer's face and tried to remember where she had seen him.

Horror gripped her heart when the memories resurfaced. She had been watching one of Joseph Goebbels' newsreels, trying not to scowl at the monster on the screen: Special Agent Jonas Amsel, the so-called Fox Hunter. The SS officer who was infamous for his ability to track down and capture Black Foxes. She remembered listening in secret to Black Fox Radio and grimacing as her boss announced that they had lost another brave agent to the predations of the Fox Hunter.

This was one of Heydrich's favorite stooges. The man who had arrested Anniska Engel.

A smirk bloomed on the Fox Hunter's face. "Frau Naden," he said, drawing his Luger from his side and aiming the barrel at her cross-clad chest. "Or would you prefer Black Fox Ten?"

Out of the frying pan, into the oven.

To be continued in the next Elyse Hoffman novel, *Black Fox One*.

https://www.amazon.com/dp/B0BW15KYVX

Sample Chapter

BLACK FOX ONE

Germany, 1927

"Ava!"

Ten-year-old Jonas Amsel was entirely certain that his best friend was going to kill him. He had followed Avalina Keller into the woods as he often did, but the girl had been too excited and had run ahead, leaving the boy to stumble through the thrush and desperately try to track her down.

"Ava!" he cried again, and this time he heard a musical giggle somewhere close by. Jonas perked up his ears and tottered forward, trying to figure out where she...

"*Boo!*"

Jonas let out an unbecoming shriek and nearly fell into a thornbush. Ava's laugh filled his ears, and by the time he recovered from the surprise and turned to face his oldest friend, he wasn't even angry at her anymore.

Ava was a pretty girl. She had onyx black hair that was slightly curly and would have fallen just past her shoulder if she didn't tie it up in a ponytail, black eyes that to Jonas seemed like a portion of a star-filled night sky that had been taken from the heavens and put in her irises, and a smile that could have melted ice.

The radiant dark-haired, dark-eyed girl contrasted mightily with her closest friend. Jonas Amsel was a tall, lanky boy with sand-blond hair and lapis-colored eyes. Ava's mother, Gisela Keller, always fondly said that while Ava was a roaring fireplace, Jonas was a candle: quiet, thoughtful, a boy that hated any sport where he had to be part of a team, a boy that preferred to either climb the monkey bars by himself or sit in a far corner and bury his face in a spy novel or a crossword puzzle.

Unless he was with Ava. When he was with Ava, Jonas was happy to do whatever crazy thing she wanted.

The fact that Ava was his best friend had also rendered her his only friend. The other boys would see Jonas walk home from school with her and would relentlessly jeer at him. "Jonas has a girlfriend! Jonas is in looove!"

But Jonas cared about Ava more than he could ever care about the opinions of a gaggle of boys, and besides, they weren't entirely wrong. She wasn't his girlfriend, but he *wished* she was.

Jonas couldn't remember a time he hadn't had a crush on her. His father, Dieter, was fond of telling the story of when they had met: little Ava had been sitting in the hallway of their apartment floor playing with paper bricks that she had carefully stacked into an impressive structure. Dieter had come out of his home, gripping his son by the hand. Jonas had seen Ava, wriggled out of his father's grasp, and tottered over to her with all the speed of a three-year-old with a mission. He had knocked down her tower by accident and timidly said, "I'm Jonas, you're pretty!"

Then Ava had yelled at him for being a town destroyer and slapped his face. They had been friends ever since.

Jonas didn't remember that incident. In fact, he couldn't remember a time that he hadn't known Ava. He also couldn't recall a time when Ava hadn't tried to give him a heart attack whenever she saw the opportunity.

"Ava!" Jonas yelped. "You scared me!"

Ava giggled and punched his arm. "Sorry, Dummi!" she said, which was what she had always called him, a teasing insult that didn't befit Jonas at all, him being the best student in their school.

"Ya scream funny, you sound more like a girl than me!" Ava cackled.

Jonas grumbled and felt a blush creep across his cheeks. He rubbed his arm, which was still sore from her playful punch. Her night-sky eyes shifted to his sore spot and glistened with mischief as she folded her arms over her chest and said, "Sorry, you wanna kiss to make it better?"

Jonas was entirely certain that his cheeks were on fire. "No!" he lied, knowing that she would make him suffer if he was honest. Her musical laugh made his ears ring.

"Good! Now c'mon, quit gettin' lost! Let's go!" She adjusted the bag she had slung over her shoulder and grabbed her friend's wrist. Jonas struggled to keep from crying out. Ava was abnormally tough for a little girl: her father Otto Keller had been one of the best soldiers on the front of the Great War. He had only recently been blessed with sons: a pair of twin boys, Fritz and Oskar. For a long time, he had assumed he would never be able to pass down his skills. Since the day Ava had beaten the shit out of one of her schoolmates for saying she looked like a Jew, however, her father had decided she was worthy of learning to fight despite her sex. "Better you know how to fight either way," he'd said. "Girls get into trouble as much as boys, and you can't always rely on Jonas to save you."

Jonas probably could have saved her if she'd let him, but whether it was bullies or make-believe villains they confronted during their escapades, Ava preferred to be the one to fight for herself, and she could fight for herself better than Jonas could ever hope to fight on her behalf. Jonas was able to hold his own when he joined Otto's lessons, but he lacked the viciousness that had earned Ava the playground moniker of Bärchen—Little Bear.

"Uhm...we're pretty far from town, Bärchen…"

"So?" the girl giggled. "The further the better! No chance I'll have to hear Fritz and Oskar cry!"

Jonas nodded. In truth, he was just as eager to get away from his home. He loved his father, but Dieter Amsel was a man in a perpetual state of mourning. The Amsel household had the atmosphere of a memorial: any space that wasn't taken up by pictures of Jonas' milestones was occupied by photos of Magda Amsel, who had died bringing Jonas into the world.

Typically, when Dieter was away or when the miasma of mourning grew too thick for Jonas to bear, the boy would retreat to the Kellers' house. Unfortunately, Ava's mother was at her wits end dealing with two yowling newborns, and thus he and Ava had been spending more and more time exploring outside. Last week, Jonas had been laid up with a cold, and so Ava had gone deep into the woods to scout out a new place for them to play. She had returned with a victorious grin, declaring in a secretive whisper that she had found something incredible.

Now Jonas' cold was nothing more than a minor cough, and so Ava dragged him deeper and deeper into the forest. Over thornbushes, past craggy stones, and over mossy hills until at last, she announced that they had arrived.

"This is it?" Jonas muttered. "I don't see anything."

Indeed, it seemed there wasn't anything special about this spot. Two twisted trees among a throng of small saplings. One tree was alive, sprouting leaves and covered in weeds. The other was grey and dead.

"Here, it's right..." Ava scurried to the space between the twisted trees and knelt down, feeling at the forest floor until she found what she was looking for. "Aha!"

Jonas watched with wonder as Ava grabbed a hatch handle hidden by false grass and moss. She threw open the disguised door, revealing a brick staircase leading into utter darkness.

"Here," Ava said, reaching into her bag and pulling out an electric lantern that she must have swiped from her father. She handed it to her accomplice. Jonas fumbled with the device and finally turned it on.

"Go on!" Ava cried, pushing him towards the stairs.

"Is...is it safe?" the boy muttered, obeying nonetheless and trudging down first.

"Well, there wasn't anyone here before, but I didn't have a lantern when I found it, so maybe there are dead bodies!"

"Ava!" Jonas squealed, turning and briefly flashing the light in her glistening night-sky eyes. She laughed wickedly and pushed him again, nearly sending him toppling down the stairs before she turned and shut the hatch, making it so that Jonas had no choice but to continue his descent.

They reached the bottom of the steps and found themselves in an empty bunker with brick and concrete walls covered in mold and dying moss. A few fluorescent lights dangled from the ceiling, connected by frayed wires.

"What is this place?" Jonas mumbled as they searched the underground hideaway, peeking in the myriad of rooms. No dead bodies, much to Jonas' relief and Ava's disappointment. In fact, there wasn't much of anything. Almost every room was barren save for a few that offered twin bedframes and one which had a musty mattress. No crates, no ammo, nothing. It was almost like the architect had constructed the structure only to either die or decide that it wouldn't do for whatever purpose it had been built for.

"Maybe it's from the war?" Ava suggested, kicking at the walls to test its structural integrity and finding that the Bunker was solid: the walls and roof didn't collapse right on top of the two children, anyway.

"Looks like it wasn't ever used," Jonas noted, flashing his beam on the mattress and wincing when a huge spider skittered out. "And it's strange to have something like this in the woods."

"Maybe they built it before everyone ended up in the trenches," muttered Ava. "Nobody's been here in forever, though…so now it's ours!"

"Er…what?" Jonas muttered as she ran to him, grabbing his arm and dragging him back towards the entrance hall. He nearly dropped the lantern, but before it could fall from his fingers, she grabbed it and set it on the staircase, pointing it at the wall.

"Here!" Ava reached into her bag and pulled out two black containers and two paintbrushes. Jonas immediately recognized the labels on the containers and felt his face heat up.

"Ava, those are Papa's paints!" he squeaked. "They're for his models!"

"So?" Ava cackled. "He wasn't usin' 'em."

Fair enough. Dieter Amsel hadn't had work as an architect for almost two years, and so his little model buildings had been rendered playsets for Jonas. Dieter hadn't seemed to mind, declaring with a smile that it was better they make his boy happy than sit around and collect dust. He'd probably have a similar mindset about the paint.

"Okay," sighed Jonas. "But we're gonna have to pickpocket someone tomorrow, someone with a fat wallet so we can pay Papa back."

"Done! I'll hit that Jew Goldhagen! C'mon, let's make it ours!"

The two children set about painting the walls of their newly claimed clubhouse. First, they scrawled out a simple message: PROPERTY OF JONAS AND AVA, KEEP OUT!

Ava added a warning: OR ELSE YOU'LL DIE! Then she drew a painting of a bear mauling a potential intruder, an intruder with a hooked nose and Semitic features. Jonas giggled. With paint and plenty of playtime to spare, the children made the wall their canvas.

"Is your papa going to the *Reichsparteitag* festival in Nuremberg?" Jonas asked, scrawling a swastika.

"It's backwards, Dummi!" Ava giggled, painting over Jonas' crooked cross and drawing the correct version beneath it. It was only reasonable that Jonas wouldn't be as familiar with the symbol of the Nazi Party as she: Ava's father had supported Hitler since the Nazi leader's failed

Beer Hall Putsch while Dieter Amsel had only just become an admirer.

"Papa wants to go, but he can't get off of work. Even if he could, he'd wanna stay with the babies and help Mama," Ava said. "What about your papa?"

"He said he's gonna try." Jonas dipped the brush again, somberly watching the paint drip onto the floor before the bristles touched the wall and he drew another swastika, this one facing the right way. "He doesn't have to worry about work, after all."

"Papa says Hitler'll fix everything and give everyone jobs," Ava declared.

"I hope so…"

"Don't worry! I won't ever let ya starve to death! Even if you run outta money, you can come live with us!"

"Really?" Jonas felt like a weight had been lifted off his heart.

"Yeah! But you'd have to sleep on the floor. You can't have my bed!"

"That's fine. I think it'd be fun to live together."

"You think?" Ava looked at him, her smile shining brighter than the flashlight. A speckle of paint was staining her cheek.

"Yeah, I'd definitely like to live with you," Jonas confirmed, suddenly wishing his own cheeks were paint-stained to hide his burning blush.

"When we're older, we can live together!" Ava suggested. "Hitler's gonna make everything better, so you won't have to move in because you go broke, but if you wanna live together anyway, then we'll have to wait until we're adults."

"Ah, like…married people?" Jonas squeaked, his heart hammering.

"Sure!" Ava declared. "You're the only boy I'd wanna marry. All the others are idiots."

"But you always call me Dummi…"

"You're not an *idiot*, you're my Dummi! It's different!"

"Av…"

"You wanna kiss?" Ava asked suddenly, her eyes sparkling. Jonas almost choked on his tongue.

"I! I!"

"If you wanna get married when we're older, you should get a kiss! Here, close your eyes and do this!" She puckered her lips. Jonas clutched the paintbrush so hard he almost broke it in two as his mind buzzed. A kiss? A real kiss! His instinct told him not to trust it, that it was far too good to be true, but his heart decreed that it was well worth the risk. He shut his eyes and puckered his lips.

He felt something brush against his mouth: not Ava's lips, but moist bristles. Jonas sputtered and spat, rubbing his mouth on his sleeve in an attempt to wipe off the paint Ava had smeared across his lips.

"A-va!" he gagged, and the girl cackled wickedly, leaping to her feet and grabbing the lantern.

"You're so gross!" she declared, bolting into the great chamber. Jonas grabbed a brush and chased her, dripping paint all along the Bunker's concrete floor.

"I'm gonna get you back for that!" he vowed, laughing even as he tried for a vengeful snarl.

"Can't catch me!" Ava cried, and her merciless giggles echoed about their new Bunker.

Germany, 1931

"Ava?"

Fourteen-year-old Jonas Amsel cried out for his friend as he descended into the Bunker, pausing only to shut the hatch lest someone else discover their secret spot. The lanterns were lit, which meant Ava was down there. She had fled from the schoolyard after decking Bruno Ackerman in the face. He'd taunted her for her dark hair and dark eyes, and Ava had responded with more viciousness than even she was typically wont to show. She'd swept his legs, knocking him to the pavement, and then punched him in the face until his handsome features resembled minced meat.

She had fled before the teachers or Bruno's parents could arrive on the scene. Jonas had known right away that she wouldn't be rushing home.

He found Ava sitting on one of the sleeping bags they had dragged into their hidden lair, scowling as she wrapped a bandage around her bruised knuckles. There was a trail of dried tears streaming down her cheeks. Vicious as Ava was, her fury had been borne from pain. It wasn't the first time she'd been called a Jew.

"Hey, Dummi," Ava muttered as Jonas sat beside her, drawing his knees to his chest and glancing down at her bruises. Protectiveness and affection made him want to ask if she was all right, but he knew better. She hated it when he treated her like a girl instead of a bear.

"I think he'll never smell again," Jonas said. "You definitely broke his nose."

"Easy to do," Ava huffed, tearing the bandage with her teeth and gazing down at her sloppy first-aid handiwork. "He's got some nerve calling me a Jew when he's got that big Jew nose."

She wriggled her fingers and then curled her hand into a fist, punching the air as though she wanted to strike Ackerman once more.

"So I'm expelled?" she grumbled. "Or just suspended?"

"Neither. You're not in any trouble," Jonas said, resting his cheek on his knee. "I told Herr Ackerman and Herr Weiss that I beat up Bruno."

Ava turned to him, night-sky eyes glistening. Puberty had made a childhood crush become a deathly distracting infatuation. Jonas had always known that Ava was pretty, but now every soft look she offered drove him mad.

"You did?" Ava said, and she sounded surprised. Jonas nodded.

"And they bought it?"

"Bruno ran with it. He didn't want his pa to know that he got beat up by a girl."

"Are…are you in trouble? You wanted to go to that chess contest…"

"Can't," Jonas sighed. "Maybe next year."

"Jonas!" Her freckle-flecked cheeks turned scarlet. "You shouldn't have done that!"

"It's all right, Ava," Jonas assured her.

"No, you're a good student!"

"Exactly: they went easy on me. *You* might have actually been expelled, and right before your gymnastics contest. I'll be okay."

"I…" Ava's shoulders sagged, and she gave him a smile, that beautiful smile that made his heart turn into a ball of flames. "Thanks. You're the best."

"I know." Jonas leaned against their painted wall, putting his hands behind his head and drinking in her praise. She punched his side, knocking the wind out of him.

"Oooowww!"

"You're gonna have to train more with me and Papa now!" Ava declared. "Bruno might have to try and beat you up now."

"But I didn't actually…"

"Yeah, but he *said* you did, so he'll have to challenge ya once his face gets better. *If* it gets better. For his honor, you know."

"Oh, I can handle him," Jonas said. He couldn't match Ava in terms of viciousness, but he had done well during Otto Keller's shooting and knife-wielding lessons. If Bruno Ackerman ever felt obliged to seek revenge, he'd have his work cut out for him.

"I guess. Is your papa upset?" Ava asked.

"He's not home. Left for Munich yesterday. He'll be back by the weekend."

"Oh! That's lucky, I guess! He's working for the Party, right?"

"For the *Schutzstaffel*," Jonas proclaimed with not a small amount of pride.

"Are those like…Stormtroopers?"

"Smaller, more elite. They're supposed to defend the Führer. Papa's working for the intelligence division, getting info on Jews and communists. It's real small right now: they're keeping filing cards in cigarette boxes, and Papa's boss has to keep borrowing a typewriter from another department. Has to carry it back and forth whenever he needs it."

"You mentioned your papa had a new boss! What was his name?"

"Heydrich, I think," Jonas said. "He and Papa both do horseback riding. Papa says he's a real talent, and a great fighter. The commies call him the Blond Beast. Hey, if Papa hears about my 'fight,' maybe he'll be happy: I can just say I was being like Herr Heydrich!"

"Well, beating up communists and beating up someone for calling me a Jew…it's a little different," muttered Ava, pinching a lock of her dark hair between her fingers and winding it around her hand. "Jonas, you don't think I look like a Jew, do you?"

Jonas sat upright. "No!" he cried so loud that his denial echoed about their hiding spot. "No, definitely not!"

"I have dark hair…"

"Don't let him get to you!" Jonas commanded, all but slamming his fist on the paint-splattered concrete floor. "You're not a Jew! You're prettier than any blonde in the school!"

The light that their lanterns offered wasn't great, but it was enough for him to see that Ava was blushing.

"Ass!" she said, punching his arm like she always did when he gave her a compliment. This time, however, her strike was soft, barely a brush. "But there are pretty Jews, y'know. Papa said that's why inbreeding is such a problem."

"Yeah, but pretty Jews are still evil. Then again, you're mean as Hell, so…"

She hit him again. He snickered. "I'm kidding!"

"You don't think I'm mean?"

"No, you're mean, but you're good even when you're mean, and you only hit people who deserve it."

"Like you?" She struck him again. He cackled.

"Yup!"

"You *do* deserve it. But you also deserve this."

She leaned forward too suddenly for him to think of defending himself, but this time she didn't tease or spit or lick his cheek or do anything else to ruin the moment. She planted a chaste little kiss right on his lips.

If Jonas Amsel's brain were a car, it would have combusted right then. He was entirely certain he had died and gone to Heaven. The only thought that went through his mind was *what what what Ava kiss what what.*

Another punch on his arm brought him back to life. "Hey, jerk!" Ava cried. "You've been trying all your life to get me to kiss ya and now you look like you're gonna throw up! I'm never kissing you again!"

She didn't keep that vow.

Germany, 1933

"Ava!"

Avalina Keller was every bit as vicious between the sheets as she was in every other capacity, which meant that stealing an intimate moment with Jonas at home was nearly impossible. The two of them were entirely too noisy to get away with screwing in their apartment complex.

Fortunately, they had the Bunker. And while it had been a hassle to drag a clean mattress all the way into the woods to replace the ancient moldy one that was filled with spiders, it was well worth it. They could be as vicious and noisy as they liked in the Bunker and their parents would be none-the-wiser.

They weren't being particularly noisy this time since Ava was in an affectionate mood, kissing her boyfriend deeply, breaking away barely long enough for Jonas to catch his breath and let out a delighted cry before her lips crashed against his again.

He wasn't about to complain, though. He grasped her tousled onyx hair with one hand while the other stroked her just so, earning a muffled moan from Ava as she deepened the kiss. A few more well-practiced caresses and she tumbled over the edge, at last breaking the kiss long enough to give him a chance to be noisy.

"Ava, Ava! Ah, God, Ava!"

"Jonas! *Jonas!*"

She collapsed on top of him, offering him another deep kiss before resting her cheek on his shoulder and fighting to catch her breath. Jonas sighed happily and kissed her temple.

"You're crushing me," he said after a moment, and she chuckled. The twin mattress didn't offer much space for snuggling, and so Ava was only barely able to shift herself off of her boyfriend, clinging to him tightly.

"We need an apartment," Jonas declared, chuckling as he wrapped an arm around her, saving her from falling off the bed. "Wanna get married?"

"Stop asking me that!" Ava giggled. It had been established long ago that her answer was *yes*, but the timing and circumstances would have to be more in their favor for them to actually tie the knot.

"You want me to marry you, you need a house and a job," Ava said, raking her hand through Jonas' sweaty sand-colored hair.

"You know, Bärchen, most girlfriends give pillow talk, not pillow nagging."

"It's not *nagging*, it's reality! We'll be out of school soon and I wanna move in with you! Screw in a queen bed in our house instead of the Bunker."

"Oooh, you don't like the Bunker?" chuckled Jonas. "You've staked your claim all over it."

He gestured to the wall above their heads, which was covered in graffiti, almost all of it naughty except for a few heartfelt, chase proclamations of love that Ava had scrawled on their anniversary or Jonas' birthday.

"I like the Bunker, but I wanna have a house, damn it. A *nice* house. We're not going to be neighbors once your papa buys a new house."

"Your family is moving too! Your papa got a raise!"

"About time, too! Fritz and Oskar need the space, they're driving me insane. But I want a place for just *us*. Besides a scary bunker with jimmy-rigged electricity."

She gestured to a flickering light above their head. Ava had managed to install a small generator to give their little hideout power again, but it was still a crude setup, barely better than what they had enjoyed as children.

"Once I finish school. We're still going to be close, Ava! We're practically still going to be neighbors! You're in the same cul-de-sac!"

"I know. Hm…you should join the SS." She ran her hand across his chest. "You'd look so handsome in the uniform."

"I'm not handsome right now?" Jonas teased, and Ava giggled impishly.

"Oh, you're handsomest when you're naked, but I can't show you off around town naked."

"You could *try…*" His quip earned him a light smack upside the head that made him chuckle.

"I think you'd be great in the SS," Ava said. "Besides the fact that you would look drop-dead gorgeous in the uniform, you've always loved puzzles and those detective books. Why not join your papa in the intelligence division? You could solve problems all day and get paid for it, plus you'd be serving the Führer!"

Jonas offered a thoughtful hum. In truth, he had considered it. There were certainly many upsides to the SS: prestige, respect, and yes, it would be very nice to have Ava brag about how handsome he looked in the uniform. Serving a great Cause, Hitler's Cause, the Cause that had made Germany strong, that had given hope and purpose to his father, that would be lovely.

Nevertheless, Jonas remembered how often his father had been away from home when he was a teenager and Dieter was throwing everything into the Nazi Cause. Hitler was Chancellor now, which might have made things a bit different. Perhaps Jonas could get a cushy position that would let him be a good husband to Ava and a good father to their inevitable brood of Aryan babies while he served the new Reich.

If not, however, he would rather become a postman and be able to come home early to Ava every day. He couldn't count the number of times he'd heard Dieter mutter that he wished he'd spent more time with Magda. Jonas wouldn't let his country get between him and Ava.

"Maybe," he said. "If I can get a flexible job. Someone will have to watch the children when you're winning gold medals at the Olympics."

"Ah, good point," Ava sighed, nestling against him and tracing his bicep with her finger. "We'll have to wait until *after* the Olympics to get married."

"You've got to be the center of the world on your wedding day, eh?"

"Damn right! Then a honeymoon…Paris?"

"Rome."

"Done. Then babies."

"We could start on the babies now if you'd just stop taking those damn pills."

"No, no, no! I've got six gymnastics competitions! I may not be going to the Olympics, but I'm gonna get close!"

"You'll be in the Olympics one day," Jonas said.

"I'm sure, and by then we'll have a litter of babies! Not now, though. Jesus, Dummi, you're suicidal. If you got me pregnant, Papa would kill you. He loves you, but he'd still kill you."

"Oh, I don't doubt it…hey!"

Ava suddenly threw her leg over him, straddling him once more.

"Don't rush," she said, pressing her lips to his cheek. "Marriage certificate or not, we're together."

"Right…" Jonas muttered, smiling as he reached up and cupped her face in his hands. "God, I love you."

She kissed him deeply in response and he felt whole. Little bits of uncertainty dotted his path—the SS? A simple civilian life? Tiny potholes to be filled in later. He had Ava. As long as he had her, he was happy.

Germany, 1936

"AVA?!"

Nineteen-year-old Jonas Amsel clutched a small ring box in one black-gloved hand and brushed the leaves and thorns that clung to his SS uniform away as he descended the staircase. He hadn't been in the Bunker for a very long time. No need: he and Ava had been living together for the past year, since Jonas had finally joined the SS and they'd bought an old fixer-upper house barely a block from the cul-de-sac where the Kellers and Dieter resided.

Life was good. He was already up for a promotion, the Olympics had been dazzling, and now it was time. A few weeks ago, Jonas had bought a golden ring with a swastika in place of a diamond and told his father that he was finally going to propose.

"About damn time!" Dieter had laughed, clapping his son's shoulder and sparing a glance at the portrait of Magda that hung on his wall. "You'll give her a wedding for the ages?"

"You think Heydrich would attend?"

"If I can drag him away from his desk for a few minutes! Between running security for the Olympics and everything else, he's a busy man! Maybe I could convince him to be your firstborn's godfather—that would be a real honor!"

Jonas had nodded in agreement, grinning at the thought of finally having a child. He had been spending his few free moments looking down at the little ring and eagerly envisioning showing off his beautiful *wife* and perfect firstborn child to the rest of the SS men. He had been waiting practically his entire life to marry Ava and now that the day was close, so close that he could already hear the wedding bells, he felt like he was going to explode from excitement.

"Ava's my Magda, Papa," Jonas had declared, glancing at his mother's eternally smiling visage. "I want to give her everything she deserves."

"I know, my boy..." Dieter had said, squeezing his son's shoulder proudly. "Don't you worry: I'll handle all the boring paperwork and submit all the family trees to *Reichsführer* Himmler. Maybe *he'll* be able to attend the wedding! Ah, then again, her father will want it to be a Christian ceremony and I *know* Himmler won't like that, you know how he is about his Nordic paganism."

Everything had been planned out after that. Dieter would submit the paperwork, Jonas would set the mood. A nice dinner, a walk about town, and then he would propose to her at night, when the star-filled sky matched her eyes, beneath the fluttering swastika banners in the middle of town square.

Jonas had been ready. He had waited at the restaurant, brimming with happiness. Everything was going so well. He was an up-and-coming SS man, Reinhard Heydrich had called him a promising recruit, the Reich was rising, and he would soon be married to the woman he loved, the woman he had *always* loved. Visions of Rome and holding his firstborn and cheering with his children as Ava claimed a gold medal for Germany at the next Olympics had danced in his head even as the minutes ticked by.

At first, he hadn't worried. Ava was always late. Late to

class, late to parties, late to church. Always late. Never *too* late, but always late.

But when minutes had turned to hours, his excitement had morphed into worry. Jonas had waited some more, but dread had gnawed at his heart until he had set off to find her.

The Kellers' house was the first place Jonas had checked. He feared that something had happened: one of her brothers had finally fallen out of a tree and gotten hurt, or her mother had an accident, something terrible that had required her immediate attention.

Jonas had arrived at the Keller abode and found their door open. He had taken out his gun, prepared to fend off an invader, but he'd walked in and discovered that the house was empty. Not completely empty: a few of the Kellers' most prized possessions were gone, along with some of their coats and clothes, but everything else was still in place. Fritz had even left behind his favorite toy sword.

Jonas had run to his father's house, knowing that if something had happened, Ava would have left word with his father.

"The Kellers are gone?" Dieter had mused. "Strange. I know nothing about this."

"You…you don't think they were arrested, do you?"

It was an odd thought: Otto Keller was a loyal National Socialist. He would sooner cut off his own tongue than speak ill of Hitler or his Cause.

"I'm sure I would have known about that," Dieter had declared, his tone gentle, the sort he had used when Jonas had been little and he'd assured the boy that there were no monsters under his bed. "Let's wait and see. Perhaps they had a family emergency."

"No, no, she would have told me, I have to..."

Jonas had run out then, still clutching the ring, and torn the town apart searching for his beloved. The hospital yielded nothing. The men at Gestapo headquarters announced that they hadn't touched the Kellers. Nothing at Fritz and Oskar's school. Nothing. They were gone, all of them...

"Ava!"

He ran down the stairs of the Bunker, his last hope for finding her. He threw on the lights and dashed down the old paint-stained halls, the chill of the Bunker eating into his very marrow when he found nothing.

Gone. She was gone.

His knees gave out, and he collapsed to the ground, clutching the ring close to his chest as ice slunk into his heart and terror tore at his soul.

"Ava..."

A note to my readers...

Thank you for reading *The Vengeance of Samuel Val*! If you enjoyed it, please tell your friends. I'd love to hear your thoughts on *The Vengeance of Samuel Val*, and reviews help authors a great deal, so I'd be very grateful if you would post a short review on Amazon and/or Goodreads. If you'd like to read more stories like this and get notifications about free and discounted books and short stories, follow me on Twitter, Facebook, Amazon, and sign up for my newsletter at elysehoffman.com! You can also follow me on Bookbub!

Historical Notes

The burning of Khruvina is based upon several similar incidents which occurred during the Second World War, most prominently the Khatyn Massacre conducted by the SS Dirlewanger Brigade and the Jedwabne Pogrom.

In the case of the former, the Khatyn Massacre, on March 22nd of 1943, troops from the infamous SS Dirlewanger "anti-partisan" brigade attacked the Belorussian village of Khatyn in retaliation for a nearby partisan attack that resulted in the deaths of four German officers.[1] The Nazis, along with their collaborators, forced the villagers into a barn which, after an hour, was lit on fire. 149 people died in this massacre, leaving only six survivors.[2] This incident was most famously semi-dramatized in the Russian film *Come and See*.

In the case of the latter, the Jedwanbe Pogrom was not directly conducted by the Nazi forces, although, as noted by historian Jan T. Gross, "[the Germans were] the undisputed bosses of life and death in Jedwabne."[3] Despite this, the massacre itself was perpetrated by Polish gentile residents, who declared, "We have to destroy all the Jews, none should stay alive."[4] After prolonged torture, beatings, and humiliation, the Jews of Jedwabne, about 300 in number including children and infants, were herded into a barn which was locked and set on fire.[5]

It should be noted that these two incidents only represent the inspiration for this particular story, and many similar events occurred throughout the Second World War.

---

1. Ingrao, C., & Green, P. (2013, July 1). *The SS Dirlewanger Brigade: The History of the Black Hunters.* Skyhorse.
2. Solly, M. (2021, March 22). *How the 1943 Khatyn Massacre Became a Symbol of Nazi Atrocities on the Eastern Front.* Smithsonian Magazine. https://www.smithsonianmag.com/history/how-1943-khatyn-massacre-became-symbol-nazi-atrocities-eastern-front-180977280/
3. Gross, J. T. (2022, April 26). *Neighbors: The Destruction of the Jewish Community in Jedwabne, Poland.* Princeton University Press.
4. *The Massacre in Jedwabne.* Copyright 2022. https://www.jewishvirtualli brary.org/the-massacre-in-jedwabne
5. *Id.*

.

Printed in Great Britain
by Amazon